Mme. Du Hausset

The Private Memoirs of Louis XV.

Mme. Du Hausset

The Private Memoirs of Louis XV.

ISBN/EAN: 9783744662789

Printed in Europe, USA, Canada, Australia, Japan

Cover: Foto ©Raphael Reischuk / pixelio.de

More available books at **www.hansebooks.com**

THE PRIVATE MEMOIRS

OF

LOUIS XV

TAKEN FROM THE MEMOIRS OF

MADAME DU HAUSSET

LADY'S MAID TO MADAME DE POMPADOUR

NUNQUAM SATIS

LONDON

H. S. NICHOLS & CO.

3 SOHO SQUARE AND 62A PICCADILLY W

MDCCCXCV

PUBLISHERS' NOTE

THE present most interesting work is the fourth in our Collection of Court Memoirs, and we do not think it necessary to give any reason for including it. for this volume of the Memoirs of Louis XV., taken from the Private Memoirs of Madame du Hausset, was bound to have a place found for it in the series.

We may remind our subscribers that the original and only editions of these works. from which we are reprinting. are forgotten. almost unknown, and unprocurable. and we experience the utmost difficulty in searching out and unearthing them ; but the remarkable success of the volumes already published has been so exceptional that we have decided to continue issuing further volumes of equal, and even surpassing interest. with the intention of eventually making this collection the best which can ever be formed.

The fifth work, which will be issued during next month, is of the utmost importance and interest, being the *Secret History of the Court of Berlin, or The Character of the present King of Prussia (Frederick William II.), his Ministers, Mistresses, Generals, Courtiers, Favourites, and the Royal Family of Prussia*, with numerous anecdotes of the Potentates of Europe, especially of the late Frederic II., by Count Mirabeau.

LONDON,

   5*th March*, 1895.

ADVERTISEMENT

[FROM THE LONDON MAGAZINE, NO. III. NEW SERIES, P. 439.]

WE were obliged by circumstances, at one time, to read all the published memoirs relative to the reign of Louis XV., and had the opportunity of reading many others which may not see the light for a long time yet to come, as their publication at present would materially militate against the interest of the descendants of the writers; and we have no hesitation in saying that the Memoirs of Madame du Hausset are the only perfectly sincere ones, amongst all those we know. Sometimes, Madame du Hausset mistakes, through ignorance, but never does she wilfully mislead, like Madame Campan, nor keep back a secret, like Madame Roland, and MM. Bezenval and Ferreires; nor is she ever betrayed by her vanity to invent, like the Duke de Lauzun, MM. Talleyrand, Bertrand de Moleville, Marmontel, Madame d'Epinay, &c. When Madame du Hausset is found in contradiction with other memoirs of the same period, we should never hesitate to give her account the preference. Whoever is desirous of accurately knowing the reign of Louis XV. should run over the very wretched history of Lacretelle, merely for the dates, and afterwards read the two

b

hundred pages of the naïve du Hausset, who, in every half page, overturns half a dozen mis-statements of this hollow rhetorician. Madame du Hausset was often separated from the little and obscure chamber in the Palace of Versailles, where resided the supreme power, only by a slight door or curtain, which permitted her to hear all that was said there. She had for a *cher ami* the greatest practical philosopher of that period, Dr. Quesnay, the founder of political economy. He was physician to Madame de Pompadour, and one of the sincerest and most single-hearted of men probably in Paris at the time. He explained to Madame du Hausset many things that, but for his assistance, she would have witnessed without understanding.

INTRODUCTION

A FRIEND of M. de Marigny (the brother of Madame de Pompadour) called on him one day and found him burning papers. Taking up a large packet, which he was going to throw into the fire—" This," said he, "is the journal of a waiting-woman of my sister's. She was a very estimable person, but it is all gossip: to the fire with it!" He stopped, and added, "Don't you think I am a little like the curate and the barber burning Don Quixote's romances."—" I beg for mercy on this," said his friend. " I am fond of anecdotes, and I shall be sure to find some here which will interest me."—" Take it, then," said M. de Marigny, and gave it him.

The hand-writing and the spelling of this journal are very bad. It abounds in tautology and repetitions; facts are sometimes inverted in the order of time; but to remedy all these defects it would have been necessary to recast the whole, which would have completely changed the character of the work. The spelling and punctuation were, however, corrected in the original, and some explanatory notes added.

Madame de Pompadour had two waiting-women of good family. The one, Madame du Hausset, who did not change her name; and another, who assumed a name, and did not publicly announce her quality. This journal is evidently the production of the former.

The amours of Louis XV. were, for a long time, covered with the veil of mystery. The public talked of the Parc-aux-Cerfs, but were acquainted with none of its details. Louis XIV. who, in the early part of his reign, had endeavoured to conceal his attachments, towards the close of it gave them a publicity which in one way increased the scandal; but his mistresses were all women of quality, entitled by their birth to be received at Court. Nothing can better describe the spirit of the time, and the character of the Monarch, than these words of Madame de Montespan: " He does not love me," said she, " but he thinks he owes it to his subjects, and to his own greatness, to have the most beautiful woman in his kingdom as his mistress."

PRIVATE MEMOIRS

OF

LOUIS XV

AND MEMOIRS OF MADAME DU HAUSSET

AN early friend of mine, who married well at
Paris, and who has the reputation of being a very
clever woman, has often asked me to write down
what daily passed under my notice : to please
her, I made little notes, of three or four lines
each, to recall to my memory the most singular
or interesting facts ; as, for instance—*attempt to
assassinate the King ; he orders Madame de Pompadour to leave the Court ; M. de Machault's ingratitude, &c.* I always promised my friend that I

I

would, some time or other, reduce all these materials into the form of a regular narrative. She mentioned the " Recollections of Madame de Caylus," which were, however, not then printed : and pressed me so much to produce a similar work, that I have taken advantage of a few leisure moments to write this, which I intend to give her, in order that she may arrange it and correct the style. I was for a long time about the person of Madame de Pompadour, and my birth procured for me respectful treatment from herself, and from some distinguished persons who conceived a regard for me. I soon became the intimate friend of Doctor Quesnay, who frequently came to pass two or three hours with me.

His house was frequented by people of all parties, but the number was small, and restricted

to those who were on terms of the greatest intimacy with him. All subjects were handled with
the utmost freedom, and it is infinitely to his
honour and theirs that nothing was ever repeated.

The Countess D—— also visited me.
She was a frank and lively woman, and much
liked by Madame de Pompadour. The Baschi
family paid me great attention. M. de Marigny
had received some little services from me, in the
course of the frequent quarrels between him and
his sister, and he had a great friendship for me.
The King was in the constant habit of seeing me ;
and an accident, which I shall have occasion to
relate, rendered him very familiar with me. He
talked without any constraint when I was in the
room. During Madame de Pompadour's illness
I scarcely ever left her chamber, and passed the

night there. Sometimes, though rarely, I accompanied her in her carriage with Doctor Quesnay, to whom she scarcely spoke a word, though he was a man of great talents. When I was alone with her, she talked of many affairs which nearly concerned her, and she once said to me, "The King and I have such implicit confidence in you, that we look upon you as a cat, or a dog, and go on talking as if you were not there." There was a little nook, adjoining her chamber, which has since been altered, where she knew I usually sat when I was alone, and where I heard everything that was said in the room, unless it was spoken in a low voice. But when the King wanted to speak to her in private, or in the presence of any of his ministers, he went with her into a closet, by the side of the chamber, whither she also retired when she had secret business with the

ministers, or with other important persons: as.
for instance, the Lieutenant of Police, the Postmaster-General, &c. All these circumstances brought
to my knowledge a great many things which probity will neither allow me to tell or to record. I
generally wrote without order of time, so that a
fact may be related before others which preceded
it. Madame de Pompadour had a great friendship
for three ministers: the first was M. de Machault,
to whom she was indebted for the regulation of
her income, and the payment of her debts. She
gave him the seals, and he retained the first place
in her regard till the attempt to assassinate the
King. Many people said that his conduct on
that occasion was not attributable to bad intentions; that he thought it his duty to obey the
King without making himself in any way a party
to the affair, and that his cold manners gave him

the appearance of an indifference which he did not feel. Madame de Pompadour regarded him in the light of a faithless friend ; and, perhaps, there was some justice on both sides. But for the Abbé de Bernis, M. de Machault might, probably, have retained his place.

The second minister, whom Madame de Pompadour liked, was the Abbé de Bernis. She was soon disgusted with him when she saw the absurdity of his conduct. He gave a singular specimen of this on the very day of his dismissal. He had invited a great many people of distinction to a splendid entertainment, which was to have taken place on the very day when he received his order of banishment, and had written in the notes of invitation—*M. Le Comte de Lusace will be there.* This Count was the brother of the Dauphiness, and this mention of him was deservedly thought impertinent. The King said, wittily enough, "*Lambert and Moliere will be there.*" She scarcely ever spoke of Cardinal de Bernis after his dismissal from the Court.

He was extremely ridiculous, but he was a good sort of man. Madame, the Infanta, died a little time before, and, by the way, of such a complication of putrid and malignant diseases, that the capuchins who bore the body, and the men who committed it to the grave, were over-powered by the effluvia. Her papers appeared no less impure in the eyes of the King. He discovered that the Abbé de Bernis had been intriguing with her, that they had deceived him, and had obtained the Cardinal's hat by making use of his name. The King was so indignant that he was very near refusing him the *barette*. He did grant it—but just as he would have thrown a bone to a dog. The Abbé had always the air of a protégé when he was in the company of Madame de Pompadour. She had known him in positive distress. The Duke de Choiseul was very differently situated ; his birth, his air, his manners, gave him claims to consideration, and he far exceeded every other man in the art of ingratiating himself with Madame de Pompadour. She looked upon him as one of the most illustrious nobles of the Court, as the most able minister, and the most agreeable man. M. de Choiseul had a sister and a wife, whom he had introduced to her, and who sedulously cultivated her favourable sentiments towards him. From the time he was minister, she saw only with his eyes ; he had the talent of amusing her, and his manners to women, generally, were extremely agreeable.

Two persons — the Lieutenant of Police and the Postmaster - General — were very much in Madame de Pompadour's confidence ; the latter, however, became less necessary to her from the time that the King communicated to M. de Choiseul the secret of the post-office, that is to say, the system of opening letters and extracting matter from them : this had never been imparted to M. d'Argenson, in spite of the high favour he enjoyed. I have heard that M. de Choiseul abused the confidence reposed in him, and related to his friends the ludicrous stories, and the love affairs, contained in the letters which were broken open. The plan they pursued, as I have heard, was very simple. Six or seven clerks of the post-office picked out the letters they were ordered to break open, and took the impression of the seals with a ball of quicksilver.

They then put each letter, with the seal down-
wards, over a glass of hot water, which melted
the wax without injuring the paper.   It was then
opened, the desired matter extracted, and it was
sealed again, by means of the impression. This is
the account of the matter I have heard.   The
Postmaster-General carried the extracts to the
King on Sundays.   He was seen coming and
going on this noble errand as openly as the
ministers. Doctor Quesnay often, in my presence,
flew in such a rage about that *infamous* minister,
as he called him, that he foamed at the mouth.
" I would as soon dine with the hangman as with
the Postmaster-General," said the Doctor.   It
must be acknowledged that this was astonishing
language to be uttered in the apartments of the
King's mistress; yet it went on for twenty
years without being talked of.   " It was probity

speaking with earnestness," said M. de Marigny, "and not a mere burst of spite or malignity."

The Duke de Gontaut was the brother-in-law and friend of M. de Choiseul, and was assiduous in his attendance on Madame de Pompadour. The sister of M. de Choiseul, Madame de Grammont, and his wife were equally constant in their attentions. This will sufficiently account for the ascendancy of M. de Choiseul, whom nobody would have ventured to attack. Chance, however, discovered to me a secret correspondence of the King, with a man in a very obscure station. This man, who had a place in the *fermes generales,* of from two to three hundred a-year, was related to one of the young ladies of the *parc aux cerfs,* by whom he was recommended to the King. He was also connected in some way with M. de Broglie, in whom the King placed great con-

fidence. Wearied with finding that his correspondence procured him no advancement, he took
the resolution of writing to me, and requesting an
interview, which I granted, after acquainting Madame de Pompadour with the circumstance. After
a great deal of preamble and of flattery, he said
to me, "Can you give me your word of honour,
and that of Madame de Pompadour, that no mention whatever of what I am going to tell you will
be made to the King?"—"I think I can assure
you, that, if you require such a promise from
Madame de Pompadour, and if it can produce no
ill consequences to the King's service, she will
give it you." He gave me his word that what he
requested would have no bad effect; upon which
I listened to what he had to say. He shewed me
several memorials, containing accusations of M. de
Choiseul, and revealed some curious circumstances

relative to the secret functions of the Count de Broglie. These, however, led rather to conjectures than to certainty, as to the nature of the services he rendered to the King. Lastly, he shewed me several letters in the King's handwriting. " I request," said he. "that the Marchioness de Pompadour will procure for me the place of Receiver-General of Finances : I will give her information of whatever I send the King : I will write according to her instructions, and I will send her his answers." As I did not choose to take liberties with the King's papers, I only undertook to deliver the memorials. Madame de Pompadour having given me her word according to the conditions on which I had received the communication, I revealed to her everything I had heard. She sent the memorials to M. de Choiseul, who thought them very maliciously and very cleverly written.

Madame de Pompadour and he had a long conference as to the reply that was to be given to the
person by whom those disclosures were made.
What I was commissioned to say was this: that
the place of Receiver-General was at present too
important, and would occasion too much surprise
and speculation; that it would not do to go beyond
a place worth seven or eight hundred a-year; that
they had no desire to pry into the King's secrets;
and that his correspondence ought not to be communicated to any one: that this did not apply to
papers like those of which I was the bearer, which
might fall into his hands; that he would confer
an obligation by communicating them, in order
that blows aimed in the dark, and directed by
malignity and imposture, might be parried. The
answer was respectful and proper, in what related
to the King: it was, however, calculated to counter-

act the schemes of the Count de Broglie, by making M. de Choiseul acquainted with his attacks, and with the nature of the weapons he employed. It was from the Count that he received statements relating to the war and to the navy; but he had no communication with him concerning foreign affairs, which the Count, as it was said, transacted immediately with the King. The Duke de Choiseul got the man who spoke to me recommended to the Controllor-General, without his appearing in the business: he had the place which was agreed upon, and the hope of a still better, and he entrusted to me the King's correspondence, which I told him I should not mention to Madame de Pompadour, according to her injunctions. He sent several memorials to M. de Choiseul, containing accusations of him, addressed to the King. This timely information enabled him to refute them triumphantly.

The King was very fond of having little private correspondences, very often unknown to Madame de Pompadour : she knew, however, of the existence of some, for he passed part of his mornings in writing to his family, to the King of Spain, to Cardinal Tencin, to the Abbé de Broglie, and also to some obscure persons. " It is, doubtless, from such people as these," said she to me, one day, "that the King learns expressions which perfectly surprise me. For instance, he said to me yesterday, when he saw a man pass with an old coat on, ' *il y a là un habit bien examiné.*' He once said to me, when he meant to express that a thing was probable, '*il y a gros* '; I am told this is a saying of the common people, meaning, *il y a gros à parier.*" I took the liberty to say, " But is it not

more likely from his young ladies at the Parc,
that he learns these elegant expressions?" She
laughed, and said, "You are right; *il y a gros.*"
The King, however, used these expressions de-
signedly, and with a laugh.

The King knew a great many anecdotes, and
there were people enough who furnished him with
such as were likely to mortify the self-love of
others. One day, at Choisy, he went into a room
where some people were employed about em-
broidered furniture, to see how they were going
on : and looking out of the window, he saw at
the end of a long avenue two men in the Choisy
uniform. "Who are those two noblemen?" said
he. Madame de Pompadour took up her glass,
and said, "They are the Duke d'Aumont, and
———." "Ah!" said the King: "the Duke
d'Aumont's grandfather would be greatly asto-

nished if he could see his grandson arm in arm
with the grandson of his valet de chambre,
L——, in a dress which may be called a patent
of nobility ! " He went on to tell Madame de
Pompadour a long history, to prove the truth of
what he said. The King went out to accompany
her into the garden ; and, soon after, Quesnay and
M. de Marigny came in. I spoke with contempt
of someone who was very fond of money. At this
the Doctor laughed, and said, " I had a curious
dream last night : I was in the country of the
ancient Germans ; I had a large house, stacks of
corn, herds of cattle, a great number of horses,
and huge barrels of ale ; but I suffered dreadfully
from rheumatism, and knew not how to manage
to go to a fountain, at fifty leagues' distance, the
waters of which would cure me. I was to go
among a strange people. An enchanter appeared

before me, and said to me, 'I pity your distress :
here, I will give you a little packet of the powder
of *prelinpinpin ;* whoever receives a little of this
from you, will lodge you, feed you, and pay you
all sorts of civilities.' I took the powder, and
thanked him."—"Ah ! " said I, " how I should
like to have some powder of *prelinpinpin!* I wish I
had a chest full." " Well," said the Doctor, "that
powder is *money*, for which you have so great a
contempt. Tell me who, of all the men who
come hither, receives the greatest attentions ? "
" I do not know," said I. " Why," said he, " it
is M. de Monmartel, who comes four or five
times a year." " Why does he enjoy so much
consideration ? " " Because his coffers are full
of the powder of *prelinpinpin.* Everything in existence," said he, taking a handful of louis from
his pocket, " is contained in these little pieces of

metal, which will convey you commodiously from one end of the world to the other. All men obey those who possess this powder, and eagerly tender them their services. To despise money, is to despise happiness, liberty, in short, enjoyments of every kind." A *cordon bleu* passed under the window. "That nobleman," said I, "is much more delighted with his *cordon bleu* than he would be with ten thousand of your pieces of metal." "When I ask the King for a pension," replied Quesnay, "I say to him, 'Give me the means of having a better dinner, a warmer coat, a carriage to shelter me from the weather, and to transport me from place to place without fatigue.' But the man who asks him for that fine blue ribbon, would say, if he had the courage and the honesty to speak as he feels, 'I am vain, and it will give me great satisfaction to see the people look at me, as I pass, with an eye of stupid admiration, and make way for me: I wish, when I enter a room, to produce an effect, and to excite the attention of those who may, perhaps, laugh at me when I am gone; I wish to be called *Monseigneur* by the multitude.' Is not all this mere empty air? In scarcely any country will his ribbon be of the slightest use to him: it will give him no power. My pieces of metal will give me the power of assisting the unfortunate everywhere. Long live the omnipotent powder of *prelinpinpin!*" At these last words, we heard a burst of laughter from the adjoining room, which was only separated by a door from the one we were in. The door opened, and in came the King. Madame de Pompadour, and M. de Gontaut. "Long live the powder of *prelinpinpin!*" said the King. "Doctor, can you get me any of it?" It happened, that when the

King returned from his walk, he was struck with a fancy to listen to our conversation. Madame de Pompadour was extremely kind to the Doctor, and the King went out laughing, and talking with great admiration of the powder. I went away, and so did the Doctor. I immediately sat down to commit this conversation to writing. I was afterwards told that M. Quesnay was very learned in certain matters relating to finance, and that he was a great *économiste*. But I do not know very well what that means. What I do know for certain is, that he was very clever, very gay and witty, and a very able physician.

The illness of the little Duke of Burgundy, whose intelligence was much talked of, for a long time occupied the attention of the Court. Great endeavours were made to find out the cause of his malady, and ill-nature went so far as to

assert that his nurse, who had an excellent situation at Versailles, had communicated to him a
nasty disease. The King shewed Madame de
Pompadour the information he had procured from
the province she came from, as to her conduct.
A silly bishop thought proper to say she had
been very licentious in her youth. The poor
nurse was told of this, and begged that he might
be made to explain himself. The bishop replied,
that she had been at several balls in the town
in which she lived, and that she had gone with
her neck uncovered. The poor man actually
thought this the height of licentiousness. The
King, who had been at first uneasy, when he
came to this, called out, "*What a fool!*" After
having long been a source of anxiety to the Court,
the Duke died. Nothing produces a stronger impression upon princes, than the spectacle of their

equals dying. Everybody is occupied about them while ill—but as soon as they are dead, nobody mentions them. The King frequently talked about death—and about funerals, and places of burial. Nobody could be of a more melancholy temperament. Madame de Pompadour once told me that he experienced a painful sensation whenever he was forced to laugh, and that he had often begged her to break off a droll story. He smiled, and that was all. In general, he had the most gloomy ideas concerning almost all events. When there was a new minister, he used to say. "*He displays his wares like all the rest, and promises the finest things in the world, not one of which will be fulfilled He does not know this country—he will see.*" When new projects for reinforcing the navy were laid before him, he said, " This is the twentieth time I have heard this talked of—

France never will have a navy, I think." This I heard from M. de Marigny.

I never saw Madame de Pompadour so re-joiced as at the taking of Mahon. The King was very glad, too, but he had no belief in the merit of his courtiers—he looked upon their success as the effect of chance. Marshal Saxe was, as I have been told, the only man who inspired him with great esteem. But he had scarcely ever seen him in his closet, nor playing the courtier.

M. d'Argenson picked a quarrel with M. de Richelieu, after his victory, about his return to Paris. This was intended to prevent his coming to enjoy his triumph. He tried to throw the thing upon Madame de Pompadour, who was enthusiastic about him, and called him by no other name than the "Minorcan." The Chevalier de Montaign was the favourite of the Dauphin,

and much beloved by him for his great devotion.
He fell ill, and underwent an operation called
l'empième, which is performed by making an
incision between the ribs, in order to let out
the pus; it had, to all appearance, a favourable
result, but the patient grew worse, and could
not breathe. His medical attendants could not
conceive what occasioned this accident and re-
tarded his cure. He died almost in the arms
of the Dauphin, who went every day to see
him. The singularity of his disease determined
the surgeons to open the body, and they found,
in his chest, part of the leaden syringe with
which decoctions had, as was usual, been in-
jected into the part in a state of suppuration.
The surgeon, who committed this act of negli-
gence, took care not to boast of his feat, and
his patient was the victim. This incident was

much talked of by the King, who related it, I
believe, not less than thirty times, according to
his custom; but what occasioned still more conversation about the Chevalier de Montaign, was
a box, found by his bed's side, containing hair-
cloths, and shirts, and whips, stained with blood.
This circumstance was spoken of one evening at
supper, at Madame de Pompadour's, and not one
of the guests seemed at all tempted to imitate
the Chevalier.   Eight or ten days afterwards, the
following tale was sent to the King, to Madame
de Pompadour, to the Baschi, and to the Duke
d'Ayen.   At first, nobody could understand to
what it referred: at last, the Duke d'Ayen exclaimed, " How stupid we are: this is a joke on
the austerities of the Chevalier de Montaign!"
This appeared clear enough—so much the more
so, as copies were sent to the Dauphin, the

Dauphiness, the Abbé de St. Cyr, and to the Duke de V——. The latter had the character of a pretender to devotion, and, in his copy, there was this addition, "*You would not be such a fool, my dear Duke, as to be a faquir — confess that you would be very glad to be one of those good monks who lead such a jolly life.*" The Duke de Richelieu was suspected of having employed one of his wits to write the story. The King was scandalised at it, and ordered the Lieutenant of Police to endeavour to find out the author, but either he could not succeed or he would not betray him.

Japanese Tale.

At a distance of three leagues from the capital of Japan, there is a temple celebrated for the concourse of persons, of both sexes, and of all ranks, who crowd thither to worship an idol be-

lieved to work miracles. Three hundred men con-
secrated to the service of religion, and who can
give proofs of ancient and illustrious descent,
serve this temple, and present to the idol the
offerings which are brought from all the provinces of the empire. They inhabit a vast and
magnificent edifice, belonging to the temple, and
surrounded with gardens where art has combined
with nature to produce enchantment. I obtained
permission to see the temple, and to walk in
the gardens. A monk advanced in years, but
still full of vigour and vivacity, accompanied me.
I saw several others, of different ages, who were
walking there. But what surprised me was to
see a great many of them amusing themselves by
various agreeable and sportive games with young
girls elegantly dressed, listening to their songs,
and joining in their dances. The monk, who

accompanied me, listened with great civility and kindness to the questions I put to him concerning his order. The following is the sum of his answers to my numerous interrogations. The God Faraki, whom we worship, is so called from a word which signifies the *fabricator*. He made all that we behold—the earth, the stars, the sun, &c. He has endowed men with senses, which are so many sources of pleasure, and we think that the only way of shewing our gratitude is to use them. This opinion will, doubtless, appear to you much more rational than that of the faquirs of India, who pass their lives in thwarting nature, and who inflict upon themselves the most melancholy privations and the most severe sufferings.

As soon as the sun rises, we repair to the mountain you see before us, at the foot of which, flows a stream of the most limpid water, which meanders in graceful windings through that meadow—enamelled with the loveliest flowers. We gather the most fragrant of them, which we carry and lay upon the altar, together with various fruits, which we receive from the bounty of Faraki. We then sing his praises, and execute dances expressive of our thankfulness, and of all the enjoyments we owe to this beneficent deity. The highest of these is that which love produces, and we testify our ardent gratitude by the manner in which we avail ourselves of this inestimable gift of Faraki. Having left the temple, we go into several shady thickets, where we take a light repast ; after which, each of us employs himself in some unoppressive labour. Some embroider, others apply themselves to painting, others cultivate flowers or fruits, others turn little implements for our use. Many of these little works

are sold to the people, who purchase them with
eagerness. The money arising from this sale,
forms a considerable part of our revenue. Our
morning is thus devoted to the worship of God
and to the exercise of the sense of sight, which
begins with the first rays of the sun. The sense
of Taste is gratified by our dinner, and we add
to it the pleasure of Smell. The most delicious
viands are spread for us in apartments strewed
with flowers. The table is adorned with them,
and the most exquisite wines are handed to us in
crystal goblets. When we have glorified God,
by the agreeable use of the palate, and the olfac-
tory nerve, we enjoy a delightful sleep of two
hours, in bowers of orange trees, roses, and myr-
tles. Having acquired a fresh store of strength
and spirits, we return to our occupations, that we
may thus mingle labour with pleasure, which

would lose its zest by long continuance. After our work, we return to the temple, to thank God, and to offer him incense. From thence we go to the most delightful part of the garden, where we find three hundred young girls, some of whom form lively dances with the younger of our monks; the others execute serious dances, which require neither strength nor agility, and which only keep time to the sound of musical instruments.

We talk and laugh with our companions, who are dressed in a light gauze, and whose tresses are adorned with flowers; we press them to partake of exquisite sherbets, differently prepared. The hour of supper being arrived, we repair to rooms illuminated with the lustre of a thousand tapers fragrant with amber. The supper-room is surrounded by three vast galleries, in which are placed musicians, whose various instruments fill

3

the mind with the most pleasurable and the softest emotions. The young girls are seated at table with us, and, towards the conclusion of the repast, they sing songs, which are hymns in honour of the God who has endowed us with senses which shed such a charm over existence, and which promise us new pleasure from every fresh exercise of them. After the repast is ended, we return to the dance, and, when the hour of repose arrives, we draw from a kind of lottery, in which every one is sure of a prize ; that is, a young girl as his companion for the night. They are allotted thus by chance, in order to avoid jealousy, and to prevent exclusive attachments. Thus ends the day, and gives place to a night of delights, which we sanctify by enjoying with due relish that sweetest of all pleasures, which Faraki has so wisely attached to the reproduction of our species.

We reverently admire the wisdom and the goodness of Faraki, who, desiring to secure to the
world a continued population, has implanted in
the sexes an invincible mutual attraction, which
constantly draws them towards each other.
Fecundity is the end he proposes, and he
rewards with intoxicating delights those who
contribute to the fulfilment of his designs.
What should we say to the favourite of a King
from whom he had received a beautiful house,
and fine estates, and who chose to spoil the
house, to let it fall in ruins, to abandon the
cultivation of the land, and to let it become
sterile, and covered with thorns? Such is the
conduct of the Faquirs of India, who condemn
themselves to the most melancholy privations,
and to the most severe sufferings. Is not this
insulting Faraki? Is it not saying to him, I

despise your gifts? Is it not misrepresenting
him and saying, You are malevolent and cruel,
and I know that I can no otherwise please
you than by offering you the spectacle of my
miseries? "I am told," added he, "that you
have, in your country, Faquirs not less insane,
not less cruel to themselves." I thought, with
some reason, that he meant the fathers of La
Trappe. The recital of the matter afforded me
much matter for reflection, and I admired how
strange are the systems to which perverted
reason gives birth.

The Duke de V——— was a nobleman of
high rank and great wealth. He said to the
King one evening at supper, "Your Majesty does
me the favour to treat me with great kindness:
I should be inconsolable if I had the misfortune
to fall under your displeasure. If such a

calamity were to befall me, I should endeavour to divert my grief by improving some beautiful estates of mine in such and such a province;" and he thereupon gave a description of three or four fine seats. About a month after, talking of the disgrace of a minister, he said, "I hope your Majesty will not withdraw your favour from me; but if I had the misfortune to lose it, I should be more to be pitied than anybody, for I have no asylum in which to hide my head." All those present, who had heard the description of the beautiful country houses, looked at each other and laughed. The King said to Madame de Pompadour, who sat next him at table, "*People are very right in saying that a liar ought to have a good memory.*"

An event, which made me tremble, as well as Madame, procured me the familiarity of the

King. In the middle of the night, Madame came into my chamber, *en chemise*, and in a state of distraction : " Here ! Here ! " said she, " the King is dying." My alarm may be easily imagined. I put on a petticoat, and found the King in her bed, panting. What was to be done ?—it was an indigestion. We threw water upon him, and he came to himself. I made him swallow some Hoffman's drops, and he said to me, " Do not make any noise, but go to Quesnay; say that your mistress is ill; and tell the doctor's servants to say nothing about it." Quesnay, who lodged close by, came immediately, and was much astonished to see the King in that state. He felt his pulse, and said, " The crisis is over; but, if the King were sixty years old, this might have been serious." He went to seek some drug, and, on his return, set

about inundating the King with perfumed water.
I forget the name of the medicine he made
him take, but the effect was wonderful. I
believe it was the *drops of General Lamotte.* I
called up one of the girls of the wardrobe to
make tea, as if for myself. The King took
three cups, put on his robe de chambre and
his stockings, and went to his own room,
leaning upon the doctor. What a sight it was
to see us all three half naked! Madame put
on a robe as soon as possible, and I did the
same, and the King changed his clothes behind
the curtains, which were very decently closed.
He afterwards spoke of this short attack, and
expressed his sense of the attentions shown
him. An hour after, I felt the greatest possible
terror in thinking that the King might have
died in our hands. Happily, he quickly recovered

himself, and none of the domestics perceived
what had taken place. I merely told the girl
of the wardrobe to put everything to rights,
and she thought it was Madame who had been
indisposed. The King, the next morning, gave
secretly to Quesnay a little note for Madame,
in which he said, *Ma chère amie must have had
a great fright, but let her re-assure herself—I am
now well, which the Doctor will certify to you.*
From that moment the King became accustomed
to me, and, touched by the interest I had
shown for him, he often gave me one of his
peculiarly gracious glances, and made me little
presents, and, on every New Year's Day, sent
me porcelain to the amount of twenty *louis
d'or*. He told Madame that he looked upon
me in the apartment as a picture or statue,
and never put any constraint upon himself

on account of my presence. Doctor Quesnay received a pension of a thousand crowns for his attention and silence, and the promise of a place for his son. The King gave me an order upon the Treasury for four thousand francs, and Madame had presented to her a very handsome chiming-clock and the King's portrait in a snuff-box.

The King was habitually melancholy, and liked everything which recalled the idea of death, in spite of the strongest fears of it. Of this, the following is an instance. Madame de Pompadour was on her way to Crécy, when one of the King's grooms made a sign to her coachman to stop, and told him that the King's carriage had broken down, and that, knowing her to be at no great distance, his Majesty had sent him forward to beg her to wait for him. He soon overtook us,

and seated himself in Madame de Pompadour's
carriage, in which were, I think, Madame de
Château-Rénaud, and Madame de Mirepoix. The
lords in attendance placed themselves in some
other carriages. I was behind, in a chaise, with
Gourbillon, Madame de Pompadour's valet de
chambre. We were surprised in a short time by
the King stopping his carriage. Those which
followed, of course stopped also. The King called
a groom, and said to him, "You see that little
eminence; there are crosses; it must certainly be
a burying ground; go and see whether there are
any graves newly dug." The groom galloped up
to it, returned, and said to the King, "There are
three quite freshly made." Madame de Pompadour, as she told me, turned away her head
with horror; and the little *Maréchale*[1] gaily said,

---

[1] The Maréchale de Mirepoix died at Brussels, in 1791;

"*This is indeed enough to make one's mouth water.*"
Madame de Pompadour spoke of it when I was
undressing her in the evening. "What a strange
pleasure!" said she, "to endeavour to fill one's
mind with images which one ought to endeavour
to banish, especially when one is surrounded by
so many sources of happiness! But that is the
King's way; he loves to talk about death. He
said, some days ago, to M. de Fontanieu, who was
seized with a bleeding at the nose, at the levée,
'Take care of yourself; at your age it is a fore-

_____

at a very advanced age, but preserving her wit and gaiety
to the last. The day of her death, after she had received
the Sacrament, the Physician told her that he thought her
a good deal better. She replied, "You tell me bad news:
having packed up, I had rather go." She was sister of
the Prince de Beauveau. The Prince de Ligne says, in
one of his printed letters, " She had that enchanting talent
which supplies the means of pleasing everybody. You
would have sworn that she had thought of nothing but you
all her life.'—ED.

runner of apoplexy.' The poor man went home frightened, and absolutely ill."

I never saw the King so agitated as during the illness of the Dauphin. The physicians came incessantly to the apartments of Madame de Pompadour, where the King interrogated them. There was one from Paris, a very odd man, called Pousse, who once said to him, " You are a good papa ; I like you for that. But you know we are all your children, and share your distress. Take courage, however ; your son will recover." Everybody's eyes were upon the Duke of Orleans, who knew not how to look. He would have become heir to the crown, the Queen being past the age to have children. Madame de —— said to me, one day, when I was expressing my surprise at the King's grief, " It would annoy him beyond measure to have a prince of the blood, heir apparent. He does not like them, and looks upon their relationship to him as so remote, that he would feel humiliated by it." And, in fact, when his son recovered, he said, "The King of Spain would have had a fine chance." It was thought that he was right in this, and that it would have been agreeable to justice ; but that, if the Duke of Orleans had been supported by a party, he might have supported his pretensions to the crown. It was, doubtless, to remove this impression that he gave a magnificent fête at St. Cloud on the occasion of the Dauphin's recovery. Madame de Pompadour said to Madame de Brancas, speaking of this fête, " He wishes to make us forget the *châteaux en Espagne* he has been dreaming of : in *Spain*, however, they build them of solider materials." The people did not shew so much joy at the Dau-

phin's recovery. They looked upon him as a
devotee, who did nothing but sing psalms. They
loved the Duke of Orleans, who lived in the
capital, and had acquired the name of the *King
of Paris.* These sentiments were not just ; the
Dauphin only sang psalms when imitating the
tones of one of the choristers of the chapel.
The people afterwards acknowledged their error,
and did justice to his virtues. The Duke of
Orleans paid the most assiduous court to Madame
de Pompadour : the Duchess, on the contrary,
detested her. It is possible that words were
put in the Duchess's mouth, which she never
uttered ; but she, certainly, often said most cut-
ting things. The King would have sent her into
exile, had he listened only to his resentment ;
but he feared the éclat of such a proceeding,
and he knew that she would only be the more

malicious. The Duke of Orleans was, just then, extremely jealous of the Count de Melfort ; and the Lieutenant of Police told the King, he had strong reasons for believing that the Duke would stick at nothing to rid himself of this gallant, and that he thought it his duty to give the Count notice, that he ought to be upon his guard. The King said, " He would not dare to attempt any such violence as you seem to apprehend ; but there is a better way : let him try to surprise them, and he will find me very well inclined to have his cursed wife shut up : but if he got rid of this lover, she would have another to-morrow. Nay, she has others at this moment ; for instance, the Chevalier de Colbert, and the Count de l'Aigle." Madame de Pompadour, however, told me these two last affairs were not certain.

An adventure happened about the same time, which the Lieutenant of Police reported to the King. The Duchess of Orleans had amused herself one evening, about eight o'clock, with ogling a handsome young Dutchman, whom she took a fancy to, from a window of the Palais Royal. The young man, taking her for a woman of the town, wanted to make short work, at which she was very much shocked. She called a Swiss, and made herself known. The stranger was arrested ; but he defended himself by affirming that she had talked very loosely to him. He was dismissed, and the Duke of Orleans gave his wife a severe reprimand.

The King (who hated her so much that he spoke of her without the slightest restraint) one day said to Madame de Pompadour, in my presence, " Her mother knew what she was, for,

before her marriage, she never suffered her to
say more than yes and no. Do you know her
joke on the nomination of Moras? She sent to
congratulate him upon it: two minutes after, she
called back the messenger she had sent, and
said, before everybody present, ' Before you speak
to him, ask the Swiss if he still has the place.'"
Madame de Pompadour was not vindictive, and,
in spite of the malicious speeches of the Duchess
of Orleans, she tried to excuse her conduct:
" Almost all women," said she, " have lovers;
she has not all that are imputed to her: but
her free manners, and her conversation, which is
beyond all bounds, have brought her into general
disrepute."

My companion came into my room the
other day, quite delighted. She had been with
M. de Chenevières, first Clerk in the War-office,

and a constant correspondent of Voltaire, whom she looks upon as a god. She was, by the bye, put into a great rage one day, lately, by a print-seller in the street, who was crying, " Here is Voltaire, the famous Prussian ; here you see him, with a great bear - skin cap, to keep him from the cold ! Here is the famous Prussian, for three-pence ! " " What a profanation ! " said she. To return to my story : M. de Chenevières had shewn her some letters from Voltaire, and M. Marmontel had read an *Epistle to his Library.*

M. Quesnay came in for a moment ; she told him all this : and, as he did not appear to take any great interest in it, she asked him if he did not admire great poets. " Oh, yes ; just as I admire great bilboquet players," said he, in that tone of his, which rendered everything he said diverting. " I have written some verses, however," said he, "and I will repeat them to you; they are upon a certain M. Rodot, an Intendant of the Marine, who was very fond of abusing medicine and medical men. I made these verses to revenge Æsculapius and Hippocrates.

> Antoine se medicina
>   En decriant la medicine,
> Et de ses propres mains mina
>   Les fondemens de sa machine :
> Très rarement il opina
>   Sans humeur bizarre ou chagrine,
> Et, l'esprit qui le domina
>   Etait affiché sur sa mine.

What do you say to them ? " said the Doctor. My companion thought them very pretty, and the Doctor gave me them in his handwriting, begging me, at the same time, not to give any copies.

Madame de Pompadour joked my companion about her *bel-esprit*, but sometimes she reposed

confidence in her.   Knowing that she was often
writing, she said to her, " You are writing a novel,
which will appear some day or other; or, perhaps,
the age of Louis XV. : I beg you to treat me
well." I have no reason to complain of her. It
signifies very little to me that she can talk more
learnedly than I can about prose and verse.

She never told me her real name; but one
day I was malicious enough to say to her, " Someone was maintaining, yesterday, that the family of
Madame de Mar—— was of more importance than
many of good extraction.   They say it is the first
in Cadiz.   She had very honourable alliances, and
yet she has thought it no degradation to be governess to Madame de Pompadour's daughter.   One
day, you will see her sons or her nephews *farmers
general*, and her grand - daughters married to
Dukes."   I had remarked that Madame de Pom-

padour for some days had taken chocolate, *à triple vanille et ambré*, at her breakfast; and that she ate truffles and celery soup: finding her in a very heated state, I one day remonstrated with her about her diet, to which she paid no attention. I then thought it right to speak to her friend, the Duchess de Brancas. "I had remarked the same thing," said she, "and I will speak to her about it before you." After she was dressed, Madame de Brancas, accordingly, told her she was uneasy about her health. "I have just been talking to her about it," said the Duchess, pointing to me. "and she is of my opinion." Madame de Pompadour seemed a little displeased; at last, she burst into tears. I immediately went out, shut the door, and returned to my place to listen. "My dear friend," said she to Madame de Brancas. "I am agitated by the fear of losing the King's heart by ceasing to be attractive to him. Men, you know, set great value on certain things, and I have the misfortune to be of a very cold temperament. I, therefore, determined to adopt a heating diet, in order to remedy this defect, and for two days this elixir has been of great service to me, or, at least, I have thought I felt its good effects." The Duchess de Brancas took the phial which was upon the toilet, and after having smelt at it, " Fie ! " said she, and threw it into the fire. Madame de Pompadour scolded her, and said, " I don't like to be treated like a child." She wept again, and said, " You don't know what happened to me a week ago. The King, under pretext of the heat of the weather, lay down upon my sofa, and passed half the night there. He will take a disgust to me and have another mistress." — " You will not avoid that," replied the Duchess, "by following your new diet, and that diet will kill you; render your company more and more precious to the King by your gentleness: do not repulse him in his fond moments, and let time do the rest; the chains of habit will bind him to you for ever." They then embraced; Madame de Pompadour recommended secresy to Madame de Brancas, and the diet was abandoned.

A little while after, she said to me, "Our master is better pleased with me. This is since I spoke to Quesnay, without, however, telling him all. He told me, that to accomplish my end, I must try to be in good health, to digest well, and, for that purpose, take exercise. I think the Doctor is right. I feel quite a different creature. I adore that man (the King), I wish so earnestly to be agreeable to him! But, alas!

sometimes he says I am a *macreuse* (a cold-blooded aquatic bird). I would give my life to please him."

One day, the King came in very much heated. I withdrew to my post, where I listened. " What is the matter ? " said Madame de Pompadour. " The long robes and the clergy," replied he, " are always at drawn daggers, they distract me by their quarrels. But I detest the long robes the most. My clergy, on the whole, is attached and faithful to me ; the others want to keep me in a state of tutelage."—" Firmness," said Madame de Pompadour, " is the only thing that can subdue them."—" Robert Saint Vincent is an incendiary, whom I wish I could banish, but that would make a terrible tumult. On the other hand, the Archbishop is an iron - hearted fellow, who tries to pick quarrels. Happily, there are some in the

parliament upon whom I can rely, and who affect
to be very violent, but can be softened upon occasion.   It costs me a few abbeys, and a few secret
pensions, to accomplish this.   There is a certain
V—— who serves me very well, while he appears to be furious on the other side." — "I can
tell you some news of him, Sire," said Madame
de Pompadour.   "He wrote to me yesterday, pre-
tending that he is related to me, and begging
for an interview." — "Well," said the King, "let
him come.   See him; and if he behaves well, we
shall have a pretext for giving him something."
M. de Gontaut came in, and seeing that they
were talking seriously, said nothing.   The King
walked about in an agitated manner, and suddenly
exclaimed, "The Regent was very wrong in restoring to them the right of remonstrating : they
will end in ruining the State."—"Ah, sire," said

M. de Gontaut, "it is too strong to be shaken by a set of petty justices."—"You don't know what they do, nor what they think. They are an assembly of republicans; however, here is enough of the subject. Things will last as they are as long as I shall. Talk about this on Sunday, Madame, with M. Berrier." Madame d'Amblimont and Madame d'Esparbès came in. "Ah! here come my kittens," said Madame de Pompadour; "all that we are about is Greek to them; but their gaiety restores my tranquility, and enables me to attend again to serious affairs. You, Sire, have the chase to divert you—they answer the same purpose to me."—The King then began to talk about his morning's sport, and Lansmatte.[1]

It was necessary to let the King go on upon these subjects, and even, sometimes, to hear the same story three or four times over, if new persons came into the room. Madame de Pompadour never betrayed the least ennui. She even sometimes persuaded him to begin his story anew.

I one day said to her, "It appears to me, Madame, that you are fonder than ever of the Countess d'Amblimont." — "I have reason to be so," said she. "She is unique, I think, for her fidelity to her friends, and for her honour. Listen, but tell nobody—four days ago, the King, passing her to go to supper, approached her, under the pretence of tickling her, and tried to slip a note into her hand. D'Amblimont, in her madcap way, put her hands behind her back, and the King was obliged to pick up the note, which had fallen on the ground. Gontaut was the only per-

son who saw all this, and, after supper, he went
up to the little lady, and said, " You are an
excellent friend."—" I did my duty," said she,
and immediately put her finger on her lips to
enjoin him to be silent. He, however, informed
me of this act of friendship of the little heroine,
who had not told me of it herself. I admired
the Countess's virtue, and Madame de Pompadour
said, " She is giddy and headlong; but she has
more sense and more feeling than a thousand
prudes and devotees. D'Esparbès would not do
as much—most likely she would meet him more
than half-way. The King appeared disconcerted,
but he still pays her great attentions."—" You
will, doubtless, Madame," said I, "shew your
sense of such admirable conduct."—" You need
not doubt it," said she, " but I don't wish her
to think that I am informed of it." The King,

prompted either by the remains of his liking, or from the suggestions of Madame de Pompadour, one morning went to call on Madame d'Ambli-mont, at Choisy, and threw round her neck a collar of diamonds and emeralds, worth between two and three thousand pounds. This happened a long time after the circumstance I have just related.

There was a large sofa in a little room adjoining Madame de Pompadour's, upon which I often reposed.

One evening, towards midnight, a bat flew into the apartment where the Court was; the King immediately cried out, "Where is General Crillon?" (He had just left the room.) He is the General to command against the bats." This set everybody calling out, "*où étais tu, Crillon?*" M. Crillon soon after came in, and

was told where the enemy was. He immediately
threw off his coat, drew his sword, and com-
menced an attack upon the bat, which flew into
the closet where I was fast asleep. I started out
of sleep at the noise, and saw the King and all
the company around me. This furnished amusement for the rest of the evening. M. de Crillon
was a very excellent and agreeable man, but
he had the fault of indulging in buffooneries of
this kind, which, however, were the result of his
natural gaiety, and not of any subserviency of
character. Such, however, was not the case with
another exalted nobleman, a Knight of the
Golden Fleece, whom Madame saw one day
shaking hands with her valet de chambre. As
he was one of the vainest men at Court,
Madame could not refrain from telling the
circumstance to the King; and, as he had no

employment at Court, the King scarcely ever after named him on the Supper List.

I had a cousin at Saint Cyr, who was married. She was greatly distressed at having a relation waiting woman to Madame de Pompadour, and often treated me in the most mortifying manner. Madame knew this from Colin,[1] her steward, and spoke of it to the King. "I am not surprised at it," said he—"this is a specimen of the silly women of Saint Cyr. Madame de Maintenon had excellent intentions, but she made a great mistake. These girls are brought up in such a manner, that, unless they are all made ladies of the palace, they are unhappy and impertinent."

1 Colin was a *procureur* of the Châtelet, who was entrusted with the favourite's affairs, and decorated, by her desire, with the Cross of St. Louis, by means of an office in the order.

Some time after, this relation of mine was at
my house. Colin, who knew her, though she did
not know him, came in. He said to me, " Do
you know that the Prince de Chimay has made
a violent attack upon the Chevalier d'Henin for
being equerry to the Marchioness." At these
words, my cousin looked very much astonished,
and said, " Was he not right ? "—" I don't mean
to enter into that question," said Colin—" but
only to repeat his words, which were these : ' If
you were only a man of moderately good family
and poor, I should not blame you, knowing, as
I do, that there are hundreds such, who would
quarrel for your place, as young ladies of family
would, to be about your mistress. But, recollect,
that your relations are princes of the empire, and
that you bear their name.' "—" What, sir," said
my relation, " the Marchioness's equerry of a

princely house ? " —" Of the house of Chimay,"
said he; "they take the name of Alsace "—witness the cardinal of that name. Colin went out
delighted at what he had said.

" I cannot get over my surprise at what I
have heard," said my relation. " It is, nevertheless, very true," replied I ; " you may see the
Chevalier d'Henin (that is the family name of
the Princes de Chimay), with the cloak of
Madame upon his arm, and walking alongside
her sedan-chair, in order that he may be ready,
on her getting in, to cover her shoulders with
her cloak, and then remain in the anti-chamber,
if there is no other room, till her return."

From that time, my cousin let me alone ;
nay, she even applied to me to get a company of
horse for her husband, who was very loth to come
and thank me. His wife wished him to thank

5

Madame de Pompadour; but, the fear he had lest
she should tell him, that it was in consideration
of his relationship to her waiting-woman that he
commanded fifty horse, prevented him.   It was,
however, a most surprising thing, that a man
belonging to the house of Chimay should be in
the service of any lady whatever; and the com-
mander of Alsace returned from Malta on purpose
to get him out of Madame de Pompadour's house-
hold.   He got him a pension of a hundred louis
from his family, and the Marchioness gave him a
company of horse.   The Chevalier d'Henin had
been page to the Marshal de Luxembourg, and
one can hardly imagine how he could have put
his relation in such a situation; for, generally
speaking, all great houses keep up the consequence
of their members.   M. de Machault, the Keeper
of the Seals, had, at the same time, as equerry,

a Knight of St. Louis, and a man of family—the Chevalier de Peribuse—who carried his portfolio, and walked by the side of the chair.

Whether it was from ambition, or from tenderness, Madame de Pompadour had a regard for her daughter,[1] which seemed to proceed from the bottom of her heart. She was brought up like a princess, and, like persons of that rank, was called by her Christian name alone. The first persons at Court had an eye to this alliance, but her mother had, perhaps, a better project. The King had a son by Madame de Vintimille, who resembled him in face, gesture, and manners. He was called the Count du ————. Madame de Pompadour had him brought to Bellevue.—Colin, her steward, was employed to find means to persuade his tutor to

1 The daughter of Madame de Pompadour and her husband, M. d'Etioles. She was called Alexandrine.

bring him thither. They took some refreshment
at the house of the Swiss, and the Marchioness,
in the course of her walk, appeared to meet them
by accident. She asked the name of the child,
and admired his beauty. Her daughter came up
at the same moment, and Madame de Pompadour led them into a part of the garden where
she knew the King would come. He did come,
and asked the child's name. He was told, and
looked embarrassed when Madame, pointing to
them, said they would be a beautiful couple. The
King played with the girl, without appearing to
take any notice of the boy, who, while he was
eating some figs and cakes which were brought,
his attitudes and gestures were so like those of
the King, that Madame de Pompadour was in the
utmost astonishment. "Ah!" said she, "Sire,
look at ———." " At what?" said he. "Nothing,"

replied Madame, "except that one would think one saw his father."

"I did not know," said the King, smiling, "that you were so intimately acquainted with the Count du L———." "You ought to embrace him," said she, "he is very handsome." "I will begin, then, with the young lady," said the King, and embraced them in a cold, constrained manner. I was present, having joined Mademoiselle's governess. I remarked to Madame, in the evening, that the King had not appeared very cordial in his caresses. "That is his way," said she; "but do not those children appear made for each other? If it was Louis XIV., he would make a Duke du Maine of the little boy; I do not ask so much; but a place and a dukedom for his son is very little: and it is because he is his son that I prefer him to all the little dukes of the Court. My grandchildren would blend the resemblance of their grandfather and grandmother; and this combination, which I hope to live to see, would, one day, be my greatest delight." The tears came into her eyes as she spoke. Alas! alas! only six months elapsed, when her darling daughter, the hope of her advanced years, the object of her fondest wishes, died suddenly. Madame de Pompadour was inconsolable, and I must do M. de Marigny the justice to say that he was deeply afflicted. His niece was beautiful as an angel, and destined to the highest fortunes, and I always thought that he had formed the design of marrying her. A dukedom would have given him rank; and that, joined to his place, and to the wealth which she would have had from her mother, would have made him a man of great importance. The difference of age was not sufficient to be a great obstacle. People, as usual, said the young lady was poisoned : for the unexpected death of persons who command a large portion of public attention always gives birth to these rumours. The King shewed great regret, but more for the grief of Madame than on account of the loss itself, though he had often caressed the child, and loaded her with presents. I owe it, also, to justice, to say that M. de Marigny, the heir of all Madame de Pompadour's fortune, after the death of her daughter, evinced the sincerest and deepest regret every time she was seriously ill. She, soon after, began to lay plans for his establishment. Several young ladies of the highest birth were thought of ; and, perhaps, he would have been made a duke, but his turn of mind indisposed him for schemes either of marriage or

ambition.   Ten times he might have been made
Prime Minister, yet he never aspired to it.   " That
is a man," said Quesnay to me, one day, " who
is very little known ; nobody talks of his talents
or acquirements, nor of his zealous and efficient
patronage of the arts : no man, since Colbert,
has done so much in his situation : he is, moreover, an extremely honourable man, but people will
not see in him anything but the brother of the
favourite ; and, because he is fat, he is thought
dull and heavy."   This was all perfectly true.
M. de Marigny had travelled in Italy with very
able artists, and had acquired taste, and much
more information than any of his predecessors
had possessed.   As for the heaviness of his air, it
only came upon him when he grew fat ; before
that, he had a delightful face.   He was then as
handsome as his sister.   He paid court to nobody,

had no vanity, and confined himself to the society of persons with whom he was at his ease. He went rather more into company at Court after the King had taken him to ride with him in his carriage, thinking it then his duty to shew himself among the courtiers.

Madame called me, one day, into her closet, where the King was walking up and down in a very serious mood. "You must," said she, "pass some days in a house in the avenue of St. Cloud, whither I shall send you. You will there find a young lady about to lie in." The King said nothing, and I was mute from astonishment. "You will be mistress of the house, and preside, like one of the fabulous goddesses, at the *accouchement*. Your presence is necessary, in order that everything may pass secretly, and according to the King's wish. You will be present at the baptism, and name the father and mother." The King began to laugh, and said, " The father is a very honest man ; " Madame added, " beloved by every-one, and adored by those who know him." Madame then took from a little cupboard a small box, and drew from it an aigrette of diamonds, at the same time saying to the King, " I have my reasons for it not being handsomer." " It is but too much so," said the King ; " how kind you are ; " and he then embraced Madame, who wept with emotion, and, putting her hand upon the King's heart, said, " This is what I wish to secure." The King's eyes then filled with tears, and I also began weeping, without knowing why. Afterwards, the King said, " Guimard will call upon you every day, to assist you with his advice, and at the critical moment you will send for him. You will say that you expect the sponsors, and a moment after you will pretend to have received a letter, stating that they cannot come. You will, of course, affect to be very much embarrassed ; and Guimard will then say, that there is nothing for it but to take the first comers. You will then appoint as godfather and godmother some beggar, or chairman, and the servant girl of the house, and to whom you will give but twelve francs, in order not to attract attention." "A louis," added Madame, "to obviate anything singular, on the other hand." "It is you who make me economical, under certain circumstances," said the King. "Do you remember the hackney-coachman? I wanted to give him a louis, and the Duke d'Ayen said, You will be known; so that I gave him a crown." He was going to tell the whole story. Madame made a sign to him to be silent, which he obeyed, not without considerable reluctance. She afterwards told me that, at the time of the fêtes given on occasion of the Dauphin's marriage, the King came to see her at her mother's house in a hackney-coach. The coachman would not go on, and the King would have given him a louis. "The police will hear of it, if you do," said the Duke d'Ayen, "and its spies will make inquiries, which will, perhaps, lead to a discovery."

"Guimard," continued the King, "will tell you the names of the father and mother; he will be present at the ceremony, and make the usual presents. It is but fair that you also should receive yours;" and, as he said this, he gave me fifty louis, with that gracious air that he could so well assume upon certain occasions, and which no person in the kingdom had but himself. I kissed his hand and wept. "You

will take care of the *accouchée*, will you not?
She is a good creature, who has not invented
gunpowder, and I confide her entirely to your
direction: my Chancellor will tell you the rest,"
he said, turning to Madame, and then quitted
the room. "Well, what think you of the part
I am playing?" asked Madame. "It is that
of a superior woman, and an excellent friend,"
I replied. "It is his heart I wish to secure,"
said she; "and all those young girls who have
no education will not run away with it from
me. I should not be equally confident were I
to see some fine woman belonging to the Court,
or the city, attempt his conquest."

I asked Madame, if the young lady knew
that the King was the father of her child? "I
do not think she does," replied she; "but, as
he appeared fond of her, there is some reason

to fear that those about her might be too ready
to tell her; otherwise," said she, shrugging her
shoulders, "she, and all the others, are told,
that he is a Polish nobleman, a relation of the
Queen, who has apartments in the castle." This
story was contrived on account of the *cordon
bleu*, which the King has not always time to
lay aside, because, to do that, he must change
his coat, and in order to account for his having
a lodging in the castle so near the King. There
were two little rooms by the side of the chapel,
whither the King retired from his apartment,
without being seen by anybody but a sentinel,
who had his orders, and who did not know
who passed through those rooms. The King
sometimes went to the Parc-aux-cerfs, or received those young ladies in the apartments I
have mentioned.

I must here interrupt my narrative, to relate a singular adventure, which is only known to six or seven persons, masters or valets. At the time of the attempt to assassinate the King, a young girl, whom he had seen several times, and for whom he had manifested more tenderness than for most, was distracted at this horrible event. The mother-abbess of the Parc-aux-cerfs perceived her extraordinary grief, and managed so as to make her confess that she knew the Polish Count was the King of France. She confessed that she had taken from his pocket two letters, one of which was from the King of Spain, the other from the Abbé de Broglie. This was discovered afterwards, for neither she nor the mother-abbess knew the names of the writers. The girl was scolded, and M. Lebel, first valet-de-chambre, who had the management of all these affairs, was

called : he took the letters, and carried them to
the King, who was very much embarrassed in
what manner to meet a person so well informed
of his condition. The girl in question, having
perceived that the King came secretly to see her
companion, while she was neglected, watched his
arrival, and, at the moment he entered with the
abbess, who was about to withdraw, she rushed
distractedly into the room where her rival was.
She immediately threw herself at the King's feet.
" Yes," said she, " you are King of all France ;
but that would be nothing to me if you were
not also monarch of my heart : do not forsake
me, my beloved sovereign ; I was nearly mad
when your life was attempted ! " The mother-
abbess cried out, " You are mad now." The
King embraced her, which appeared to restore
her to tranquility. They succeeded in getting

her out of the room, and a few days afterwards the unhappy girl was taken to a madhouse, where she was treated as if she had been insane, for some days. But she knew well enough that she was not so, and that the King had really been her lover. This lamentable affair was related to me by the mother-abbess, when I had some acquaintance with her at the time of the accouchement I have spoken of, which I never had before, nor since.

To return to my history; Madame de Pompadour said to me, "Be constantly with the *accouchée*, to prevent any stranger, or even the people of the house, from speaking to her. You will always say that he is a very rich Polish nobleman, who is obliged to conceal himself on account of his relationship to the Queen, who is very devout. You will find a wet-nurse in the house, to whom you will deliver the child. Guimard will manage

6

all the rest. You will go to church as a witness;
everything must be conducted as if for a substan-
tial citizen. The young lady expects to lie in in
five or six days; you will dine with her, and will
not leave her till she is in a state of health to
return to the Parc-aux-cerfs, which she may do in
a fortnight, as I imagine, without running any
risk." I went, that same evening, to the Avenue
de Saint Cloud, where I found the Abbess and
Guimard, an attendant belonging to the castle,
but without his blue coat. There were, besides,
a nurse, a wet-nurse, two old men-servants, and a
girl, who was something between a servant and a
waiting-woman. The young lady was extremely
pretty, and dressed very elegantly, though not too
remarkably. I supped with her and the mother-
abbess, who was called Madame Bertrand. I had
presented the aigrette Madame de Pompadour gave

me before supper, which had greatly delighted the young lady, and she was in high spirits. Madame Bertrand had been housekeeper to M. Lebel, first valet-de-chambre to the King. He called her Dominique, and she was entirely in his confidence. The young lady chatted with us after supper; she appeared to me very *naïve*. The next day, I talked to her in private. She said to me, "How is the Count?" (It was the King whom she called by this title.) "He will be very sorry not to be with me now: but he was obliged to set off on a long journey." I assented to what she said. "He is very handsome," said she, "and loves me with all his heart. He promised me an allowance; but I love him disinterestedly; and, if he would let me, I would follow him to Poland." She afterwards talked to me about her parents, and about M. Lebel, who she knew by the name of Durand. " My mother," said she, " kept a large grocer's shop, and my father was a man of some consequence ; he belonged to the Six Corps, and that, as everybody knows, is an excellent thing. He was twice very near being head-bailiff." Her mother had become bankrupt at her father's death, but *the Count* had come to her assistance, and settled upon her sixty pounds a-year, besides giving her two hundred and forty pounds down. On the sixth day, she was brought to bed, and, according to my instructions, she was told the child was a girl, though in reality it was a boy ; she was soon to be told that it was dead, in order that no trace of its existence might remain for a certain time. It was eventually to be re-stored to its mother. The King gave each of his children four or five hundred a-year. They inheri-ted after each other as they died off, and seven

or eight were already dead. I returned to Madame
de Pompadour, to whom I had written every day
by Guimard. The next day, the King sent for
me into the room ; he did not say a word as
to the business I had been employed upon ; but
he gave me a large gold snuff-box, containing two
rouleaux of twenty-five louis each. I curtsied to
him, and retired. Madame asked me a great
many questions of the young lady, and laughed
heartily at her simplicity, and at all she had said
about the Polish nobleman. " He is disgusted
with the Princess, and, I think, will return to
Poland for ever, in two months." " And the
young lady ? " said I. " She will be married in
the country," said she, " with a portion of forty
thousand crowns (7,000*l.* or 8,000*l.*) at the most,
and a few diamonds." This little adventure,
which initiated me into the King's secrets, far

from procuring for me increased marks of kindness
from him, seemed to produce a coldness towards
me; probably because he was ashamed of my
knowing his obscure amours. He was also embarrassed by the services Madame de Pompadour
had rendered him on this occasion.

Besides the little mistresses of the Parc-aux-
cerfs, the King had sometimes intrigues with
ladies of the Court, or from Paris, who wrote
to him. There was a Madame de L——, who,
though married to a young and amiable man,
with two hundred thousand francs a year, wished
absolutely to become his mistress. She contrived
to have a meeting with him: and the King,
who knew who she was, was persuaded that she
was really madly in love with him. There is no
knowing what might have happened, had she not
died. Madame was very much alarmed, and was

only relieved by her death from inquietude. A circumstance took place at this time which doubled Madame's friendship for me. A rich man, who had a situation in the Revenue Department, called on me one day very secretly, and told me that he had something of importance to communicate to Madame la Marquise, but that he should find himself very much embarrassed in communicating it to her personally, and that he should prefer acquainting me with it. He then told me, what I already knew, that he had a very beautiful wife, of whom he was passionately fond; that having on one occasion perceived her kissing a little *porte-feuille*, he endeavoured to get possession of it, supposing there was some mystery attached to it. One day that she suddenly left the room to go upstairs to see her sister, who had been brought to bed, he took the opportunity of opening the *porte-feuille*, and was very much surprised to find in it a portrait of the King, and a very tender letter written by His Majesty. Of the latter he took a copy, as also of an unfinished letter of his wife, in which she vehemently entreated the King to allow her to have the pleasure of an interview—the means she pointed out. She was to go masked to the public ball at Versailles, where His Majesty could meet her under favour of a mask. I assured M. de —— that I should acquaint Madame with the affair, who would, no doubt, feel very grateful for the communication. He then added, " Tell Madame la Marquise that my wife is very clever and very intriguing. I adore her, and should run distracted were she to be taken from me." I lost not a moment in acquainting Madame with the affair, and gave her the letter. She became serious and pensive, and I since learned that she consulted M. Berrier, Lieutenant of Police, who, by a very simple but ingeniously conceived plan, put an end to the designs of this lady. He demanded an audience of the King, and told him that there was a lady in Paris who was making free with His Majesty's name; that he had been given the copy of a letter, supposed to have been written by His Majesty to the lady in question. The copy he put into the King's hands, who read it in great confusion, and then tore it furiously to pieces. M. Berrier added, that it was rumoured that this lady was to meet His Majesty at the public ball, and, at this very moment, it so happened that a letter was put into the King's hand, which proved to be from the lady, appointing the meeting; at least, M. Berrier judged so, as the King appeared very much surprised on reading it, and said, " It must be allowed, M. le Lieutenant of Police, that you are well informed." M. Berrier added, " I think it my duty to tell Your Majesty that this lady passes for a very intriguing person." " I believe," replied the King, " that it is not without deserving it that she has got that character."

Madame de Pompadour had many vexations in the midst of all her grandeur. She often received anonymous letters, threatening her with poison or assassination : her greatest fear, how-ever, was that of being supplanted by a rival. I never saw her in a greater agitation than, one evening, on her return from the drawing-room at Marly. She threw down her cloak and muff, the instant she came in, with an air of ill-humour, and undressed herself in a hurried manner.

Having dismissed her other women, she said to me, " I think I never saw anybody so insolent as Madame de Coaslin. I was seated at the same table with her this evening, at a game of *brélan*, and you cannot imagine what I suffered. The men and women seemed to come in relays to watch us. Madame de Coaslin said two or three times, looking at me, *Va tout*, in the most insulting manner. I thought I should have fainted, when she said, in a triumphant tone, I have the *brélan* of kings. I wish you had seen her courtesy to me on parting."—" Did the King," said I, " show her particular attention ? " " You don't know him," said she ; " if he were going to lodge her this very night in my apartment, he would behave coldly to her before people, and would treat me with the utmost kindness. This is the effect of his education, for he is, by nature,

kind-hearted and frank." Madame de Pompadour's
alarms lasted for some months, when she, one
day, said to me, " That haughty Marchioness has
missed her aim ; she frightened the King by her
grand airs, and was incessantly teasing him for
money. Now you, perhaps, may not know that
the King would sign an order for forty thousand
pounds without a thought, and would give a
hundred out of his little private treasury with the
greatest reluctance. Lebel, who likes me better
than he would a new mistress in my place, either
by chance or design had brought a charming
little sultana to the Parc-aux-cerfs, who has cooled
the King a little towards the haughty Vashti, by
giving him occupation, ———— has received four
thousand pounds, some jewels, and an estate.
Jannette[1] has rendered me great service, by show-

---

[1] The Intendant of Police.

ing the King extracts from the letters broken open at the post-office, concerning the report that Madame de Coaslin was coming into favour.— The King was much impressed by a letter from an old counseilor of the Parliament, who wrote to one of his friends as follows : " It is quite as reasonable that the King should have a female friend and confidante—as that we, in our several degrees, should so indulge ourselves : but it is desirable that he should keep the one he has : she is gentle, injures nobody, and her fortune is made. The one who is now talked of will be as haughty as high birth can make her. She must have an allowance of forty thousand a-year, since she is said to be excessively extravagant ; her relations must be made dukes, governors of provinces, and marshals, and, in the end, will surround the King, and overawe the ministers."

Madame de Pompadour had this passage, which had been sent to her by M. Jannette, the Intendant of the Post, who enjoyed the King's entire confidence. He had carefully watched the King's look, while he read the letter, and he saw that the arguments of this counsellor, who was not a disaffected person, made a great impression upon him.—Some time afterwards, Madame de Pompadour said to me, " The haughty Marchioness behaved like Mademoiselle Deschamps,¹ and she is *turned off*." This was not Madame's only subject of alarm. A relation of Madame d'Estrades,² wife

1 A courtesan, distinguished for her charms, and still more so for an extraordinary proof of patriotism. At a time when the public treasury was exhausted, Mademoiselle Deschamps sent all her plate to the Mint. Louis XIV. boasted of this act of generous devotion to her country. The Duke d'Ayen made it the subject of a pleasantry, which detracted nothing from the merit of the sacrifice— but which is rather too *gai* for us to venture upon.

2 The Countess d'Estrades, a relative of M. Normand, and a flatterer of Madame de Pompadour, who brought her

to the Marquis de C——, had made the most pointed advances to the King, much more than were necessary for a man who justly thought himself the handsomest man in France, and who was, moreover, a King. He was perfectly persuaded that every woman would yield to the slightest desire he might deign to manifest. He, therefore, thought it a mere matter of course that women fell in love with him. M. de Stainville[1] had a hand in marring the success of that intrigue : and, soon afterwards, the Marchioness de C——, who was confined to her apartments at Marly, by her relations, escaped through a closet to a rendezvous, and was caught with a young

---

to Court, was secretly in the pay of the Count d'Argenson. That minister, who did not disdain *la Fillon*, from whom he extracted useful information, knew all that passed at the Court of the favourite, by means of Madame d'Estrades, whose ingratitude and perfidiousness he liberally paid.

[1] Afterwards Duke de Choiseul.

man in a corridor. The Spanish Ambassador, coming out of his apartments with flambeaux, was the person who witnessed this scene. Madame d'Estrades affected to know nothing of her cousin's intrigues, and kept up an appearance of the tenderest attachment to Madame de Pompadour, whom she was habitually betraying. She acted as spy for M. d'Argenson, in the cabinets, and in Madame de Pompadour's apartments ; and, when she could discover nothing, she had recourse to her invention, in order that she might not lose her importance with her lover. This* Madame d'Estrades owed her whole existence to the bounties of Madame, and yet, ugly as she was, she had tried to get the King away from her. One day, when he had got rather drunk at Choisy (I think, the only time that ever happened to him), he went on board a beautiful barge, whither Madame, being

ill of an indigestion, could not accompany him.
Madame d'Estrades seized this opportunity. She
got into the barge, and, on their return, as it was
dark, she followed the King into a private closet,
where he was believed to be sleeping on a couch,
and there went somewhat beyond any ordinary
advances to him. Her account of the matter to
Madame was, that she had gone into the closet
upon her own affairs, and that the King had
followed her, and had tried to ravish her. She
was at full liberty to make what story she
pleased, for the King knew neither what he
had said, nor what he had done. I shall finish
this subject by a short history concerning a
young lady. I had been, one day, to the
theatre at Compeigne. When I returned, Madame asked me several questions about the play:
whether there was much company, and whether

7

I did not see a very beautiful girl. I replied,
" That there was, indeed, a girl in a box near
mine, who was surrounded by all the young
men about the Court." She smiled, and said,
" That is Mademoiselle Dorothée : she went,
this evening, to see the King sup in public,
and to-morrow, she is to be taken to the hunt.
You are surprised to find me so well informed,
but I know a great deal more about her. She
was brought here by a Gascon, named Dubarré
or Dubarri, who is the greatest scoundrel in
France. He founds all his hopes of advancement on Mademoiselle Dorothée's charms, which
he thinks the King cannot resist. She is, really,
very beautiful. She was pointed out to me in
my little garden, whither she was taken to walk
on purpose. She is the daughter of a water-
carrier, at Strasbourg, and her charming lover

demands to be sent minister to Cologne, as a beginning."—"Is it possible, Madame, that you can have been rendered uneasy by such a creature as that?" "Nothing is impossible," replied she; "though I think the King would scarcely dare to give such a scandal. Besides, happily, Lebel, to quiet his conscience, told the King that the beautiful Dorotheé's lover is infected with a horrid disease;" and, added he, "Your Majesty would not get rid of that as you have done of scrofula." This was quite enough to keep the young lady at a distance.

"I pity you sincerely, Madame," said I, "while everybody else envies you."—"Ah!" replied she, "my life is that of the Christian, a perpetual warfare. This was not the case with the woman who enjoyed the favour of Louis XIV. Madame de la Valière suffered herself to be deceived by Madame de Montespan, but it was her own fault, or, rather, the effect of her extreme good nature. She was entirely devoid of suspicion at first, because she could not believe her friend perfidious. Madame de Montespan's empire was shaken by Madame de Fontanges, and overthrown by Madame de Maintenon; but her haughtiness, her caprices, had already alienated the King. He had not, however, such rivals as mine; it is true, their baseness is my security. I have, in general, little to fear but casual infidelities, and the chance that they may not all be sufficiently transitory for my safety. The King likes variety, but he is also bound by habit; he fears éclats, and detests manœuvring women. The little Marechale (de Mirepoix) one day said to me, ' It is your staircase that the King loves; he is accustomed to go up and down it. But, if he found another woman to whom he could talk of hunting and business as he does to you, it would be just the same to him in three days.' "

I write without plan, order, or date, just as things come into my mind; and I shall now go to the Abbé de Bernis, whom I liked very much, because he was good-natured, and treated me kindly. One day, just as Madame de Pompadour had finished dressing, M. de Noailles asked to speak to her in private. I, accordingly, retired. The Count looked full of important business. I heard their conversation, as there was only the door between us.

" A circumstance has taken place," said he, " which I think it my duty to communicate to the King; but I would not do so without first informing you of it, since it concerns one of your friends

for whom I have the utmost regard and respect.
The Abbé de Bernis had a mind to shoot, this
morning, and went, with two or three of his
people, armed with guns, into the little park,
where the Dauphin would not venture to shoot
without asking the King's permission. The guards,
surprised at hearing the report of guns, ran to
the spot, and were greatly astonished at the sight
of M. de Bernis. They very respectfully asked to
see his permission, when they found, to their
astonishment, that he had none. They begged of
him to desist, telling him, that, if they did their
duty, they should arrest him : but they must, at
all events, instantly acquaint me with the circumstance, as Ranger of the Park of Versailles. They
added, that the King must have heard the firing,
and that they begged of him to retire. The Abbé
apologized, on the score of ignorance, and assured

them that he had my permission. 'The Count de Noailles,' said they, 'could only grant permission to shoot in the more remote parts, and in the great park.'" The Count made a great merit of his eagerness to give the earliest information to Madame. She told him to leave the task of communicating it to the King to her, and begged of him to say nothing about the matter. M. de Marigny, who did not like the Abbé, came to see me in the evening; and I affected to know nothing of the story, and to hear it for the first time from him. " He must have been out of his senses," said he, " to shoot under the King's windows,"—and enlarged much on the airs he gave himself. Madame de Pompadour gave this affair the best colouring she could : the King was, nevertheless, greatly disgusted at it, and twenty times, since the Abbé's disgrace, when he passed over that part of the park, he said, " This is where the Abbé took his pleasure." The King never liked him ; and Madame de Pompadour told me one night, after his disgrace, when I was sitting up with her in her illness, that she saw, before he had been minister a week, that he was not fit for his office. " If that hypocritical Bishop," said she, speaking of the Bishop of Mirepoix, " had not prevented the King from granting him a pension of four hundred a-year, which he had promised me, he would never have been appointed ambassador. I should, afterwards, have been able to give him an income of eight hundred a-year, perhaps the place of master of the chapel. Thus he would have been happier, and I should have had nothing to regret." I took the liberty of saying that I did not agree with her. That he had yet remaining advantages, of

which he could not be deprived ; that his exile
would terminate ; and that he would then be a
Cardinal, with an income of eight thousand a-year.
" That is true," she replied ; " but I think of the
mortifications he has undergone, and of the ambition which devours him ; and, lastly, I think of
myself. I should have still enjoyed his society,
and should have had, in my declining years, an
old and amiable friend, if he had not been minister."—The King sent him away in anger, and
was strongly inclined to refuse him the hat. M.
Quesnay told me, some months afterwards, that
the Abbé wanted to be Prime Minister ; that he
had drawn up a memorial, setting forth that in
difficult crises the public good required that there
should be a *central point* (that was his expression),
towards which every thing should be directed.
Madame de Pompadour would not present the

memorial ; he insisted, though she said to him,
"*You will ruin yourself.*"   The King cast his eyes
over it, and said "'*central point,*'—that is to
say himself, he wants to be Prime Minister."
Madame tried to apologize for him, and said,
" That expression might refer to the Marshal de
Belle-Isle."—" Is he not just about to be made
Cardinal ? " said the King.   " This is a fine
manœuvre : he knows well enough that, by means
of that dignity, he would compel the ministers
to assemble at his house, and then M. l'Abbé
would be the *central point*. Wherever there is
a Cardinal in the council, he is sure, in the
end, to take the lead.   Louis XIV., for this
reason, did not choose to admit the Cardinal de
Janson into the council, in spite of his great
esteem for him.   The Cardinal de Fleury told
me the same thing.   He had some desire that

the Cardinal de Tencin should succeed him :
but his sister was such an intrigante that Cardinal de Fleury advised me to have nothing to
do with the matter, and I behaved so as to
destroy all his hopes, and to undeceive others.
M. d'Argenson has strongly impressed me with
the same opinion, and has succeeded in destroy-
ing all my respect for him." This is what the
King said, according to my friend Quesnay, who,
by the bye, was a great genius, as everybody
said, and a very lively, agreeable man. He
liked to chat with me about the country. I
had been bred up there, and he used to set me
a talking about the meadows of Normandy and
Poitou, the wealth of the farmers, and the modes
of culture. He was the best-natured man in the
world, and the farthest removed from petty intrigue. While he lived at Court, he was much

more occupied with the best manner of culti-
vating land than with anything that passed
around him. The man whom he esteemed the
most was M. de la Rivière, a Counsellor of
Parliament, who was also Intendant of Martini-
que : he looked upon him as a man of the
greatest genius, and thought him the only person
fit for the financial department of administration.

The Countess d'Estrades, who owed everything to Madame de Pompadour, was incessantly
intriguing against her. She was clever enough
to destroy all proofs of her manœuvres, but she
could not so easily prevent suspicion. Her intimate connection with M. d'Argenson gave offence
to Madame, and, for some time, she was more
reserved with her. She, afterwards, did a thing
which justly irritated the King and Madame.
The King, who wrote a great deal, had written to

Madame de Pompadour a long letter concerning an assembly of the Chambers of Parliament, and had enclosed a letter of M. Berrièr. Madame was ill, and laid these letters on a little table by her bedside. M. de Gontaut came in, and gossiped about trifles, as usual. Madame d'Amblimont also came, and stayed but very little time. Just as I was going to resume a book which I had been reading to Madame, the Countess d'Estrades entered, placed herself near Madame's bed, and talked to her for some time. As soon as she was gone, Madame called me, asked what was o'clock, and said, "Order my door to be shut, the King will soon be here." I gave the order, and returned; and Madame told me to give her the King's letter, which was on the table with some other papers. I gave her the papers, and told her there was nothing else. She was very uneasy at not finding the letter, and, after enumerating the persons who had been in the room, she said, " It cannot be the little Countess, nor Gontaut, who has taken this letter. It can only be the Countess d'Estrades :—and that is too bad." The King came, and was extremely angry, as Madame told me. Two days afterwards, he sent Madame d'Estrades into exile. There was no doubt that she took the letter ; the King's handwriting had probably awakened her curiosity. This occurrence gave great pain to M. d'Argenson, who was bound to her, as Madame de Pompadour said, by his love of intrigue. This redoubled his hatred of Madame, and she accused him of favouring the publication of a libel, in which she was represented as a worn-out mistress, reduced to the vile occupation of providing new objects to please her lover's appetite. She was characterised as superintendant of the Parc-aux-cerfs, which was said to cost hundreds of thousands of pounds a-year. Madame de Pompadour did, indeed, try to conceal some of the King's weaknesses, but she never knew one of the sultanas of that seraglio. There were, however, scarcely ever more than two at once, and often only one. When they married, they received some jewels, and four thousand pounds. The Parc-aux-cerfs was sometimes vacant for five or six months. I was surprised, some time after, at seeing the Duchess de Luynes, Lady of Honour to the Queen, come privately to see Madame de Pompadour. She afterwards came openly. One evening, after Madame was in bed, she called me, and said, " My dear, you will be delighted ; the Queen has given me the place of Lady of the Palace ; to-morrow I am to be

presented to her : you must make me look well."
I knew that the King was not so well pleased
at this as she was ; he was afraid that it would
give rise to scandal, and that it might be
thought he had forced this nomination upon the
Queen. He had, however, done no such thing.
It had been represented to the Queen, that it
was an act of heroism on her part to forget
the past ; that all scandal would be obliterated
when Madame de Pompadour was seen to belong
to the Court in an honourable manner ; and that
it would be the best proof that nothing more
than friendship now subsisted between the King
and the favourite. The Queen received her very
graciously. The devotees flattered themselves they
should be protected by Madame, and, for some
time, were full of her praises. Several of the
Dauphin's friends came in private to see her,

and some obtained promotion. The Chevalier du
Muy, however, refused to come. The King had
the greatest possible contempt for them, and
granted them nothing with a good grace. He,
one day, said of a man of great family, who
wished to be made Captain of the Guards, "He
is a double spy, who wants to be paid on both
sides." This was the moment at which Madame
de Pompadour seemed to me to enjoy the most
complete satisfaction. The devotees came to visit
her without scruple, and did not forget to make
use of every opportunity of serving themselves.
Madame de Lu—— had set them the example.
The Doctor laughed at this change in affairs, and
was very merry at the expense of the saints. "You
must allow, however, that they are consistent,"
said I, "and may be sincere."—"Yes," said he;
"but then they should not ask for anything."

One day, I was at Doctor Quesnay's, whilst Madame de Pompadour was at the theatre. The Marquis de Mirabeau[1] came in, and the conversation was, for some time, extremely tedious to me, running entirely on *net produce:* at length, they talked of other things.

Mirabeau said, " I think the King looks ill, he grows old."—" So much the worse, a thou-

---

1 The author of " L'Ami des Hommes," one of the leaders of the sect of *Economistes*, and father of the celebrated Mirabeau. After the death of Quesnay, the *Grand Master of the Order*, the Marquis de Mirabeau, was unanimously elected his successor. Mirabeau was not deficient in a certain enlargement of mind, or in acquirements, nor even in patriotism ; but his writings are enthusiastical, and show that he had little more than glimpses of the truth. The *Friend of Man* was the *enemy* of all his family. He beat his servants, and did not pay them. The reports of the law-suit with his wife, in 1775, prove that this philosopher possessed, in the highest possible degree, all the anti-conjugal qualities. It is said that his eldest son wrote two contradictory depositions, and was paid by both sides.

sand times so much the worse," said Quesnay;
"it would be the greatest possible loss to France
if he died:" and he raised his hands, and sighed
deeply. "I do not doubt that you are attached
to the King, and with reason," said Mirabeau:
"I am attached to him too: but I never saw
you so much moved."—"Ah!" said Quesnay,
"I think of what would follow." "Well, the
Dauphin is virtuous."—"Yes; and full of good
intentions; nor is he deficient in understanding;
but canting hypocrites would possess an absolute
empire over a Prince who regards them as
oracles. The Jesuits would govern the kingdom,
as they did at the end of Louis XIV.'s reign:
and you would see the fanatical Bishop of
Verdun Prime Minister, and La Vauguyon all-
powerful under some other title. The Parliaments
must then mind how they behave; they will

8—2

not be better treated than my friends the philosophers." — " But they go too far," said Mirabeau ; " why openly attack religion ? " — " I allow that," replied the Doctor ; " but how is it possible not to be rendered indignant by the fanaticism of others, and by recollecting all the blood that has flowed during the last two hundred years ? You must not then again irritate them, and revive in France the time of Mary in England. But what is done is done, and I often exhort them to be moderate; I wish they would follow the example of our friend Duclos."—" You are right," replied Mirabeau ; " he said to me a few days ago, ' These philosophers are going on at such a rate that they will force me to go to vespers and high mass ; ' but, in fine, the Dauphin is virtuous, well-informed, and intellectual."—" It is the commencement of his reign, I fear," said Quesnay, "when the imprudent proceedings of our friends will be represented to him in the most unfavourable point of view; when the Jansenists and Molinists will make common cause, and be strongly supported by the Dauphiness. I thought that M. de Muy was moderate, and that he would temper the headlong fury of the others; but I heard him say that Voltaire merited condign punishment. Be assured, Sir, that the times of John Huss and Jerome of Prague will return; but I hope not to live to see it. I approve of Voltaire having hunted down the Pompignans: were it not for the ridicule with which he covered them, that *bourgeois* Marquis would have been preceptor to the young Princes, and, aided by his brother, would have succeeded in again lighting the faggots of perse-cution." "What ought to give you confidence in

the Dauphin," said Mirabeau, "is, that, notwith-
standing the devotion of Pompignan, he turns
him into ridicule. A short time back, seeing
him strutting about with an air of inflated pride,
he said to a person, who told it to me, ' Our
friend Pompignan thinks that he is something.' "
On returning home, I wrote down this conversation.

I, one day, found Quesnay in great distress.
" Mirabeau," said he, " is sent to Vincennes, for
his work on taxation. The Farmers General
have denounced him, and procured his arrest :
his wife is going to throw herself at the feet
of Madame de Pompadour to-day." A few minutes afterwards, I went into Madame's apartment, to assist at her toilet, and the Doctor
came in. Madame said to him, " You must be
much concerned at the disgrace of your friend

Mirabeau. I am sorry for it too, for I like his brother." Quesnay replied, "I am very far from believing him to be actuated by bad intentions, Madame; he loves the King and the people." — "Yes," said she: "his *Ami des Hommes* did him great honour." At this moment the Lieutenant of Police entered, and Madame said to him, "Have you seen M. de Mirabeau's book?"—"Yes, Madame; but it was not I who denounced it?"—"What do you think of it?"—"I think he might have said almost all it contains with impunity, if he had been more circumspect as to the manner; there are, among other objectionable passages, this, which occurs at the beginning: *Your Majesty has about twenty millions of subjects; it is only by means of money that you can obtain their services, and there is no money.*" "What, is there really that,

Doctor ? " said Madame. " It is true, they are the first lines in the book, and I confess that they are imprudent ; but, in reading the work, it is clear that he laments that patriotism is extinct in the hearts of his fellow-citizens, and that he desires to rekindle it." The King entered : we went out, and I wrote down on Quesnay's table what I had just heard. I then returned to finish dressing Madame de Pompadour : she said to me, " The King is extremely angry with Mirabeau ; but I tried to soften him, and so did the Lieutenant of Police. This will increase Quesnay's fears. Do you know what he said to me to day ? The King had been talking to him in my room, and the Doctor appeared timid and agitated. After the King was gone, I said to him, 'You always seem so embarrassed in the King's presence, and yet he is so good-natured.'

'Madame,' said he, 'I left my native village at the age of forty, and I have very little experience of the world, nor can I accustom myself to its usages without great difficulty. When I am in a room with the King, I say to myself, This is a man who can order my head to be cut off; and that idea embarrasses me.' 'But do not the King's justice and kindness set you at ease?'—'That is very true in reasoning,' said he; 'but the sentiment is more prompt, and inspires me with fear before I have time to say to myself all that is calculated to allay it.'"

I got her to repeat this conversation, and wrote it down immediately, that I might not forget it.

An anonymous letter was addressed to the King and Madame de Pompadour: and, as the

author was very anxious that it should not mis-
carry, he sent copies to the Lieutenant of Police,
sealed and directed *to the King, to Madame de
Pompadour, and to M. de Marigny.* This letter
produced a strong impression on Madame, and
on the King, and still more, I believe, on the
Duke de Choiseul, who had received a similar
one. I went on my knees to M. de Marigny,
to prevail on him to allow me to copy it, that
I might show it to the Doctor. It is as follows :

" Sire—It is a zealous servant who writes to
Your Majesty. Truth is always better, particularly to kings; habituated to flattery, they see
objects only under those colours most likely to
please them. I have reflected, and read much ;
and here is what my meditations have suggested
to me to lay before Your Majesty. They have
accustomed you to be invisible, and inspired you

with a timidity which prevents you from speaking; thus all direct communication is cut off between the master and his subjects. Shut up in the interior of your palace, you are becoming every day like the emperors of the East: but see, Sire, their fate! 'I have troops,' Your Majesty will say; such, also, is their support: but, when the only security of a king rests upon his troops; when he is only, as one may say, a king of the soldiers, these latter feel their own strength, and abuse it. Your finances are in the greatest disorder, and the great majority of states have perished through this cause. A patriotic spirit sustained the ancient states, and united all classes for the safety of their country. In the present times, money has taken the place of this spirit; it has become the universal lever, and you are in want of it. A spirit of finance affects every department of the state; it reigns triumphant at Court; all have become venal; and all distinction of rank is broken up. Your ministers are without genius and capacity since the dismissal of MM. d'Argenson and de Machault. You alone cannot judge of their incapacity, because they lay before you what has been prepared by skilful clerks, but which they pass as their own. They provide only for the necessity of the day, but there is no spirit of government in their acts. The military changes that have taken place disgust the troops, and cause the most deserving officers to resign; a seditious flame has sprung up in the very bosom of the Parliaments; you seek to corrupt them, and the remedy is worse than the disease. It is introducing vice into the sanctuary of justice, and gangrene into the vital parts of the commonwealth. Would a corrupted Parliament have braved the fury of the League, in order to preserve the crown for the legitimate sovereign? Forgetting the maxims of Louis XIV., who well understood the danger of confiding the administration to noblemen, you have chosen M. de Choiseul, and even given him three departments; which is a much heavier burden than that which he would have to support as Prime Minister, because the latter has only to oversee the details executed by the Secretaries of State. The public fully appreciate this dazzling minister. He is nothing more than a *petit-maître*, without talents or information, who has a little phosphorus in his mind. There is a thing well worthy of remark, Sire; that is, the open war carried on against religion. Henceforward there can spring up no new sects, because the general belief has been shaken, that no one feels inclined to occupy himself with difference of

sentiment upon some of the articles.   The Ency-
clopedists, under pretence of enlightening mankind, are sapping the foundations of religion.   All
the different kinds of liberty are connected; the
Philosophers and the Protestants tend towards re-
publicanism, as well as the Jansenists.   The Philosophers strike at the root, the others lop the
branches; and their efforts, without being con-
certed, will one day lay the tree low.   Add to
these the Economists, whose object is political
liberty, as that of the others is liberty of worship,
and the Government may find itself, in twenty or
thirty years, undermined in every direction, and
will then fall with a crash.   If Your Majesty,
struck by this picture, but too true, should ask
me for a remedy, I should say, that it is necessary to bring back the Government to its principles, and, above all, to lose no time in restoring

order to the state of the finances, because the em-
barrassments incident to a country in a state of
debt, necessitate fresh taxes, which, after grinding
the people, induce them towards revolt. It is my
opinion, that Your Majesty would do well to appear more among your people : to shew your
approbation of useful services, and your displeasure of errors and prevarications, and neglect of
duty : in a word, to let it be seen that rewards
and punishments, appointments and dismissals,
proceed from yourself. You will then inspire gratitude, by your favours, and fear, by your re-
proaches; you will then be the object of immediate and personal attachment, instead of which,
every thing is now referred to your ministers.
The confidence in the King, which is habitual to
your people, is shewn by the exclamation, so common among them, ' Ah! if the King knew it.'

They love to believe that the King would remedy all their evils, if he knew of them. But, on the other hand, what sort of ideas must they form of kings, whose duty it is to be informed of every-thing, and to superintend everything, that con-cerns the public, but who are, nevertheless, igno-rant of every thing which the discharge of their functions requires them to know. *Rex, roi, regere, régir, conduire*—to rule, to conduct—these words sufficiently denote their duties. What would be said of a father who got rid of the charge of his children as of a burthen?

"A time will come, Sire, when the people shall be enlightened—and that time is probably approaching. Resume the reins of government, hold them with a firm hand, and act, so that it cannot be said of you, *Fœminas et scorta volvit animo et hæc principatûs præmia putat :*—Sire, if I see that my sincere advice should have produced any change, I shall continue it, and enter into more details ; if not. I shall remain silent."

Now that I am upon the subject of anonymous letters to the King, I must just mention that it is impossible to conceive how frequent they were. People were extremely assiduous in telling either unpleasant truths, or alarming lies, with a view to injure others. As an instance, I shall transcribe one concerning Voltaire, who paid great court to Madame de Pompadour when he was in France. This letter was written long after the former.

" Madame—M. de Voltaire has just dedicated his tragedy of *Tancred* to you ; this ought to be an offering of respect and gratitude : but it is, in fact, an insult, and you will form the same opinion of it as the public has done if you read

9

it with attention. You will see that this distinguished writer appears to betray a consciousness
that the subject of his encomiums is not worthy
of them, and to endeavour to excuse himself for
them to the public. These are his words: ' I
have seen your graces and talents unfold themselves from your infancy. At all periods of your
life I have received proofs of your uniform and
unchanging kindness. If any critic be found to
censure the homage I pay you, he must have a
heart formed for ingratitude. I am under great
obligations to you, Madame, and these obligations
it is my duty to proclaim.'

" What do these words really signify, unless
that Voltaire feels it may be thought extraordinary
that he should dedicate his work to a woman who
possesses but a small share of the public esteem,
and that the sentiment of gratitude must plead

his excuse? Why should he suppose that the homage he pays you will be censured, whilst we daily see dedications addressed to silly gossips who have neither rank nor celebrity, or to women of exceptionable conduct, without any censure being attracted by it?"

M. de Marigny, and Colin, Madame de Pompadour's steward, were of the same opinion as Quesnay, that the author of this letter was extremely malicious: that he insulted Madame, and tried to injure Voltaire: but that he was, in fact, right. Voltaire, from that moment, was entirely out of favour with Madame, and with the King, and he certainly never discovered the cause.[1]

1 The pretty lines, in which Voltaire says to Madame de Pompadour, speaking of Louis XV.,

"Soyez tous deux sans ennemis,
Et tous deux gardez vos conquêtes."

Could Voltaire be ignorant that these lines were thought

The King, who admired everything of the age of Louis XIV., and recollected that the Boileaus and Racines had been protected by that monarch, who was indebted to them, in part, for the lustre of his reign, was flattered at having such a man

improper, and that the daughters of Louis XV. persuaded their father to resent them ? Was Madame du Hausset ignorant, that, if Madame de Pompadour did not plead for the exile, it was because she herself was angry with him, for the following act of unguarded rashness ? Voltaire was surrounded by men jealous of the friendship manifested for him by the favourite. Far from attempting to conciliate, he amused himself with irritating them. Of course, every bold or indiscreet expression was reported. The great poet was one day at dinner with the Marchioness. She was eating a quail, which she said was plump — "*grass-ouillette.*" Voltaire approached her, and said, loud enough to be heard :

> "*Grassouillette,* entre nous, me semble un peu caillette,
> Je vous le dis tout bas, belle Pompadourette."

This was represented by her courtiers as a piece of ex-treme impertinence, and Voltaire perceived, from that day, a marked coldness in her manner. Laujon was present. The author of this note heard the circumstance from himself.

as Voltaire among his subjects. But still he feared him, and had but little esteem for him. He could not help saying, " Moreover, I have treated him as well as Louis XIV. treated Racine and Boileau. I have given him, as Louis XIV. gave to Racine, some pensions, and a place of gentleman in ordinary. It is not my fault if he has committed absurdities, and has had the pretension to become a chamberlain, to wear an order, and sup with a King. It is not the fashion in France ; and, as there are here a few more men of wit and noblemen than in Prussia, it would require that I should have a very large table to assemble them all at it." And then he reckoned upon his fingers, Maupertuis, Fontenelle, La Mothe, Voltaire, Piron, Destouches. Montesquieu, the Cardinal Polignac. — " Your Majesty forgets," said someone, " d'Alembert and Clairaut."

—"And Crébillon," said he. "And la Chaussée, and the younger Crébillon," said someone. "He ought to be more agreeable than his father."— "And there are also the Abbés Prévôt and d'Olivet."—"Pretty well," said the King; "and for the last twenty years *all that (tout cela)* would have dined and supped at my table."

Madame de Pompadour repeated to me this conversation, which I wrote down the same evening. M. de Marigny, also, talked to me about it.—"Voltaire," said he, "has always had a fancy for being ambassador, and he did all he could to make the people believe that he was charged with some political mission, the first time he visited Prussia."

The people heard of the attempt on the King's life with transports of fury, and with the greatest distress. Their cries were heard under the windows of Madame de Pompadour's apartment. Mobs were collected, and Madame feared the fate of Madame de Châteauroux. Her friends came in, every minute, to give her intelligence. Her room was, at all times, like a church: everybody seemed to claim a right to go in and out when he chose. Some came, under pretence of sympathising, to observe her countenance and manner. She did nothing but weep and faint away. Doctor Quesnay never left her, nor did I. M. de St. Florentin came to see her several times, so did the Comptroller-General, and M. Rouillé: but M. de Machault did not come. The Duchess of Brancas came very frequently. The Abbé de Bernis never left us, except to go to enquire for the King. The tears came in his eyes whenever he looked at Madame. Doctor Quesnay saw the King five or six times a-day. "There is nothing to fear," said he to Madame. "If it were anybody else, he might go to a ball." My son went the next day, as he had done the day the event occurred, to see what was going on at the Castle. He told us, on his return, that the Keeper of the Seals was with the King. I sent him back, to see what course he took on leaving the King. He came running back in half an hour, to tell me that the Keeper of the Seals had gone to his own house, followed by a crowd of people. When I told this to Madame, she burst into tears, and said, "*Is that a friend?*" The Abbé de Bernis said, "You must not judge him hastily, in such a moment as this." I returned into the drawing-room, about an hour after, when the Keeper of the Seals entered. He passed me, with his usual cold and severe look.

" How is Madame de Pompadour? " said he. " Alas! " replied I. " as you may imagine! " He passed on to her closet. Everybody retired, and he remained for half an hour. The Abbé returned, and Madame rang. I went into her room, the Abbé following me. She was in tears. " I must go, my dear Abbé," said she. I made her take some orange-flower water, in a silver goblet, for her teeth chattered. She then told me to call her equerry. He came in, and she calmly gave him her orders, to have everything prepared at her hotel. in Paris: to tell all her people to get ready to go; and to desire her coachman not to be out of the way. She then shut herself up, to confer with the Abbé de Bernis, who left her. to go to the Council. Her door was then shut, except to the ladies with whom she was particularly intimate. M. de Soubise, M. de

Gontaut, the ministers, and some others. Several ladies, in the greatest distress, came to talk to me in my room : they compared the conduct of M. de Machault with that of M. de Richelieu, at Metz. Madame had related to them the circumstances extremely to the honour of the Duke, and, by contrast, the severest satire on the Keeper of the Seals. " He thinks, or pretends to think," said she, " that the priests will be clamorous for my dismissal ; but Quesnay and all the physicians declare that there is not the slightest danger." Madame having sent for me, I saw the Maréchale de Mirepoix coming in. While she was at the door, she cried out, " What are all those trunks, Madame ? Your people tell me you are going."—" Alas ! my dear friend, such is our Master's desire, as M. de Mauchault tells me." " And what does he advise?" said the Maréchale. "That I should go without delay." During this conversation, I was undressing Madame, who wished to be at her ease on her chaise-longue. "Your Keeper of the Seals wants to get the power into his own hands, and betrays you; he who quits the field loses it." I went out. M. de Soubise entered, then the Abbé and M. de Marigny. The latter, who was very kind to me, came into my room an hour afterwards. I was alone. "She will remain," said he; "but, hush!—she will make an appearance of going, in order not to set her enemies at work. It is the little Maréchale who prevailed upon her to stay: her keeper (so she called M. de Machault) will pay for it." Quesnay came in, and, having heard what was said, with his monkey airs, began to relate a fable of a fox, who being at dinner with other beasts, persuaded one of them that his enemies were seeking him, in order that he might get possession of his share in his absence. I did not see Madame again till very late, at her going to bed. She was more calm. Things improved, from day to day, and de Machault, the faithless friend, was dismissed. The King returned to Madame de Pompadour, as usual. I learnt, by M. de Marigny, that the Abbé had been, one day, with M. d'Argenson, to endeavour to persuade him to live on friendly terms with Madame, and that he had been very coldly received. "He is the more arrogant," said he, "on account of Machault's dismissal, which leaves the field clear for him, who has more experience, and more talent: and I fear that he will, therefore, be disposed to declare *war till death.*" The next day, Madame having ordered her chaise, I was

curious to know where she was going, for she
went out but little, except to church, and to
the houses of the ministers.   I was told that she
was gone to visit M. d'Argenson.   She returned in
an hour, at farthest, and seemed very much out
of spirits.   She leaned on the chimney-piece, with
her eyes fixed on the border of it.   M. de Bernis
entered.   I waited for her to take off her cloak
and gloves.   She had her hands in her muff.
The Abbé stood looking at her for some minutes :
at last he said, " You look like a sheep in a reflecting mood."   She awoke from her reverie, and,
throwing her muff on the easy chair, replied, " It
is a wolf who makes the sheep reflect."   I went
out : the King entered shortly after, and I heard
Madame de Pompadour sobbing.   The Abbé came
into my room, and told me to bring some Hoffman's drops : the King himself mixed the draught

with sugar, and presented it to her in the kindest manner possible. She smiled, and kissed the King's hands. I left the room. Two days after, very early in the morning, I heard of M. d'Argenson's exile. It was her doing, and was, indeed, the strongest proof of her influence that could be given. The King was much attached to M. d'Argenson, and the war, then carrying on, both by sea and land, rendered the dismissal of two such ministers extremely imprudent. This was the universal opinion at the time.

Many people talk of the letter of the Count d'Argenson to Madame d'Esparbès. I give it, according to the most correct version. — " The doubtful is, at length, decided. The Keeper of the Seals is dismissed. You will be recalled, my dear Countess, and we shall be masters of the field."

It is much less generally known, that Arboulin, whom Madame calls Bou-bou, was supposed to be the person who, on the very day of the dismissal of the Keeper of the Seals, bribed the Count's confidential courier, who gave him this letter. Is this report founded on truth? I cannot swear that it is; but it is asserted that the letter is written in the Count's style. Besides, who could so immediately have invented it? It, however, appeared certain, from the extreme displeasure of the King, that he had some other subject of complaint against M. d'Argenson, besides his refusing to be reconciled with Madame. Nobody dares to show the slightest attachment to the disgraced minister. I asked the ladies who were most intimate with Madame de Pompadour, as well as my own friends, what they knew of the matter: but they knew nothing. I can understand why Madame did not let them into her confidence at that moment. She will be less reserved in time. I care very little about it, since I see that she is well, and appears happy.

The King said a thing, which did him honour, to a person whose name Madame withheld from me. A nobleman, who had been a most assiduous courtier of the Count, said, rubbing his hands with an air of great joy, " I have just seen the Count d'Argenson's baggage set out." When the King heard him, he went up to Madame, shrugged his shoulders, and said, " And immediately the cock crew."

I believe this is taken from Scripture, where Peter denies Our Lord. I confess, this circumstance gave me great pleasure. It showed that the King is not the dupe of those around him, and that he hates treachery and ingratitude."

Madame sent for me yesterday evening, at seven o'clock, to read something to her : the ladies who were intimate with her were at Paris, and M. de Gontaut ill. " The King," said she, " will stay late at the Council this evening : they are occupied with the affairs of the Parliament again." She bade me leave off reading, and I was going to quit the room, but she called out, " Stop." She rose ; a letter was brought in for her, and she took it with an air of impatience and ill-humour. After a considerable time she began to talk openly, which only happened when she was extremely vexed ; and, as none of her confidential friends were at hand, she said to me, " This is from my brother. It is what he would not have dared to say to me, so he writes. I had arranged a marriage for him with the daughter of a man of title : he appeared to be

well inclined to it, and I, therefore, pledged my
word.   He now tells me that he has made
inquiries ; that the parents are people of insup-
portable hauteur ; that the daughter is very badly
educated ; and that he knows. from authority
not to be doubted, that when she heard this
marriage discussed, she spoke of the connection
with the most supreme contempt ; that he is
certain of this fact ; and that I was still more
contemptuously spoken of than himself.   In a
word, he begs me to break off the treaty.   But
he has let me go too far ; and now he will make
these people my irreconcilable enemies.   This has
been put. in his head by some of his flatterers ;
they do not wish him to change his way of
living ; and very few of them would be received
by his wife."   I tried to soften Madame, and,
though I did not venture to tell her so, I thought

her brother right. She persisted in saying these were lies, and, on the following Sunday, treated her brother very coldly. He said nothing to me at that time: if he had, he would have embarrassed me greatly. Madame atoned for everything by procuring favours, which were the means of facilitating the young lady's marriage with a gentleman of the Court. Her conduct, two months after marriage, compelled Madame to confess that her brother had been perfectly right.

I saw my friend, Madame du Chiron. "Why," said she, "is the Marchioness so violent an enemy to the Jesuits? I assure you she is wrong. All-powerful as she is, she may find herself the worse for their enmity." I replied that 1 knew nothing about the matter. "It is, however, unquestionably a fact; and she does not feel that a word more or less might decide her fate."—"How do you mean?" said I. "Well, I will explain my-self fully," said she. "You know what took place at the time the King was stabbed: an attempt was made to get her out of the Castle instantly. The Jesuits have no other object than the salva-tion of their penitents; but they are men, and hatred may, without their being aware of it, influ-ence their minds, and inspire them with a greater degree of severity than circumstances absolutely demand. Favour and partiality may, on the other hand, induce the confessor to make great concessions; and the shortest interval may suffice to save a favourite, especially if any decent pre-text can be found for prolonging her stay at Court." I agreed with her in all she said, but I told her that I dared not touch that string. On reflecting on this conversation afterwards, I was forcibly struck with this fresh proof of the in-

trigues of the Jesuits, which, indeed, I knew well
already. I thought that, in spite of what I had
replied to Madame du Chiron, I ought to communicate this to Madame de Pompadour, for the
ease of my conscience ; but that I would abstain
from making any reflection upon it. "Your friend,
Madame du Chiron," said she, " is, I perceive,
affiliated to the Jesuits, and what she says does
not originate with herself. She is commissioned
by some reverend father, and I will know by
whom." Spies were, accordingly, set to watch her
movements, and they discovered that one father
de Saci, and, still more particularly, one father
Frey, guided this lady's conduct. "What a pity,"
said Madame to me, "that the Abbé Chauvelin
cannot know this." He was the most formidable
enemy of the reverend fathers. Madame du
Chiron always looked upon me as a Jansenist.

because I would not espouse the interests of the
good fathers with as much warmth as she did.

Madame is completely absorbed in the Abbé
de Bernis, whom she thinks capable of anything;
she talks of him incessantly. Apropos, of this
Abbé, I must relate an anecdote, which almost
makes one believe in conjurors. A year, or fifteen
months, before her disgrace, Madame de Pompadour, being at Fontainbleau, sat down to write at a
desk, over which hung a portrait of the King. While
she was shutting the desk, after she had finished
writing, the picture fell, and struck her violently
on the head. The persons who saw the accident
were alarmed, and sent for Dr. Quesnay. He
asked the circumstances of the case, and ordered
bleeding and anodynes. Just as she had been
bled, Madame de Brancas entered, and saw us all
in confusion and agitation, and Madame lying on

her chaise-longue. She asked what was the matter, and was told. After having expressed her regret, and having consoled her, she said, " I ask it as a favour of Madame, and of the King (who had just come in), that they will instantly send a courier to the Abbé de Bernis, and that the Marchioness will have the goodness to write a letter, merely requesting him to inform her what his fortune-tellers told him, and to withhold nothing from the fear of making her uneasy." The thing was done as she desired, and she then told us that La Bontemps had predicted, from the dregs in the coffee-cup, in which she read everything, that the head of her best friend was in danger, but that no fatal consequences would ensue.

The next day, the Abbé wrote word, that Madame Bontemps also said to him, " You came into the world almost black," and that this was

the fact. This colour, which lasted for some
time, was attributed to a picture which hung at
the foot of his mother's bed, and which she often
looked at. It represented a Moor bringing to
Cleopatra a basket of flowers, containing the asp
by whose bite she destroyed herself. He said
that she also told him, " You have a great deal
of money about you, but it does not belong to
you ; " and that he had actually in his pocket two
hundred louis for the Duke de la Vallière. Lastly,
he informed us that she said, looking in the cup,
" I see one of your friends—the best—a distinguished lady, threatened with an accident : " that
he confessed that, in spite of all his philosophy,
he turned pale : that she remarked this, looked
again into the cup, and continued, " Her head will
be slightly in danger, but of this no appearance will
remain half an hour afterwards. It was impossible

to doubt the facts." They appeared so surprising to the King, that he desired some inquiry to be made concerning the fortune - teller. Madame, however, protected her from the pursuit of the Police.

A man, who was quite as astonishing as this fortune-teller, often visited Madame de Pompadour. This was the Count de St. Germain, who wished to have it believed that he had lived several centuries.[1] One day, at her toilet,

---

[1] St. Germain was an adept—a worthy predecessor of Cagliostro, who expected to live five hundred years. The Count de St. Germain pretended to have already lived two thousand, and, according to him, the account was still running. He went so far as to claim the power of transmitting the gift of long life. One day, calling upon his servant to bear witness to a fact that went pretty far back, the man replied, "I have no recollection of it, sir; you forget that I have only had the honour of serving you for five hundred years."

St. Germain, like all other charlatans of this sort,

Madame said to him, in my presence, "What was the personal appearance of Francis I. ? He was a King I should have liked." — "He was, indeed, very captivating," said St. Germain; and he proceeded to describe his face and person as one does that of a man one has accurately observed. "It is a pity he was too ardent. I could have given him some good advice, which

assumed a theatrical magnificence, and an air of science calculated to deceive the vulgar. His best instrument of deception was the phantasmagoria; and as, by means of this abuse of the science of optics, he called up shades which were asked for, and almost always recognised, his correspondence with the other world was a thing proved by the concurrent testimony of numerous witnesses.

He played the same game in London, Venice, and Holland, but he constantly regretted Paris, where his miracles were never questioned.

St. Germain passed his latter days at the Court of the Prince of Hesse Cassel, and died at Plewig, in 1784, in the midst of his enthusiastic disciples, and to their infinite astonishment at his sharing the common destiny.

would have saved him from all his misfortunes ;
but he would not have followed it : for it seems
as if a fatality attended princes, forcing them to
shut their ears, those of the mind, at least, to
the best advice, and especially in the most critical moments."—" And the Constable," said Madame, " what do you say of him ? "—" I cannot
say much good or much harm of him," replied
he.   " Was the Court of Francis I. very brilliant ? "—" Very brilliant ; but those of his grand-
sons infinitely surpassed it.   In the time of Mary
Stuart and Margaret of Valois it was a land of
enchantment a temple, sacred to pleasures of
every kind : those of the mind were not neglected.
The two Queens were learned, wrote verses, and
spoke with captivating grace and eloquence."   Madame said, laughing, " You seem to have seen all
this."—" I have an excellent memory," said he,

and have read the history of France with great
care.   I sometimes amuse myself, not by *making*,
but by *letting* it be believed that I lived in old
times."—" You do not tell me your age. however,
and you give yourself out for very old. The Countess de Gergy, who was ambassadress to Venice,
I think, fifty years ago, says she knew you there
exactly what you are now."—" It is true, Madame,
that I have known Madame de Gergy a long time."
—"But, according to what she says, you would be
more than a hundred."—" That is not impossible,"
said he, laughing : " but it is, I allow, still more
possible, that Madame de Gergy, for whom I have
the greatest respect, may be in her dotage."—
" You have given her an elixir, the effect of which
is surprising.   She declares that for a long time
she has felt as if she was only four-and-twenty
years of age ; why don't you give some to the

King ? "—" Ah ! Madame," said he, with a sort of terror, " I must be mad to think of giving the King an unknown drug." I went into my room to write down this conversation.

Some days afterwards, the King, Madame de Pompadour, some Lords of the Court, and the Count de St. Germain, were talking about his secret for causing the spots in diamonds to disappear. The King ordered a diamond of middling size, which had a spot, to be brought. It was weighed ; and the King said to the Count, " It is valued at two hundred and forty pounds ; but it would be worth four hundred if it had no spot. Will you try to put a hundred and sixty pounds into my pocket ?" He examined it carefully, and said, " It may be done : and I will bring it you again in a month." At the time appointed, the Count brought back the diamond without a spot.

and gave it to the King. It was wrapped in a
cloth of amianthus, which he took off. The King
had it weighed, and found it but very little
diminished. The King sent it to his jeweller by
M. de Gontaut, without telling him anything of
what had passed. The jeweller gave three hundred and eighty pounds for it. The King, however,
sent for it back again, and kept it as a curiosity.
He could not overcome his surprise, and said
that M. de St. Germain must be worth millions,
especially if he had also the secret of making large
diamonds out of a number of small ones. He
neither said that he had, nor that he had not ;
but he positively asserted that he could make
pearls grow, and give them the finest water. The
King paid him great attention, and so did Madame
de Pompadour. It was from her I learnt what I
have just related. M. Quesnay said, talking of the

pearls. " They are produced by a disease in the oyster. It is possible to know the cause of it : but. be that as it may. he is not the less a quack. since he pretends to have the *elixir vitæ*. and to have lived several centuries. Our master is. however, infatuated by him. and sometimes talks of him as if his descent were illustrious."

I have seen him frequently : he appeared to be about fifty : he was neither fat nor thin : he had an acute. intelligent look. dressed very simply. but in good taste : he wore very fine diamonds in his rings. watch, and snuff-box. He came, one day, to visit Madame de Pompadour, at a time when the Court was in full splendour, with knee and shoe-buckles of diamonds so fine and brilliant that Madame said she did not believe the King had any equal to them. He went into the ante-chamber to take them off, and brought them to be examined; they were compared with others in the room, and the Duke de Gontaut, who was present, said, they were worth at least eight thousand pounds. He wore, at the same time, a snuffbox of inestimable value, and ruby sleeve-buttons, which were perfectly dazzling. Nobody could find out by what means this man became so rich and so remarkable; but the King would not suffer him to be spoken of with ridicule or contempt. He was said to be a bastard son of the King of Portugal.

I learnt, from M. de Marigny, that the relations of the good little *Maréchale* (de Mirepoix) had been extremely severe upon her, for what they called the baseness of her conduct, with regard to Madame de Pompadour. They said she held the stones of the cherries which Madame ate in her carriage, in her beautiful little hands, and that she sate in the front of the carriage, while Madame occupied the whole seat in the inside. The truth was, that, in going to Crécy, on an insupportably hot day, they both wished to sit alone, that they might be cooler; and as to the matter of the cherries, the villagers having brought them some, they ate them to refresh themselves, while the horses were changed; and the *Maréchale* emptied her pocket-handkerchief, into which they had both thrown the cherry-stones, out of the carriage window. The people who were changing the horses had given their own version of the affair.

I had, as you know, a very pretty room at Madame's hotel, whither I generally went privately. I had, one day, had visits from two or three Paris representatives, who told me news; and Madame, having sent for me, I went to her,

and found her with M. de Gontaut. I could not
help instantly saying to her, "You must be much
pleased, Madame, at the noble action of the Marquis de ——." Madame replied, drily, "Hold
your tongue, and listen to what I have to say to
you." I returned to my little room, where I found
the Countess d'Amblimont, to whom I mentioned Madame's reception of me. "I know what
is the matter," said she; "it has no relation to
you. I will explain it to you. The Marquis de
—— has told all Paris, that, some days ago,
going home at night, alone, and on foot, he heard
cries in a street called Férou, which is dark, and,
in great part, arched over. That he drew his
sword, and went down the street, in which he
saw, by the light of a lamp, a very handsome
woman, to whom some ruffians were offering violence; that he approached, and that the woman

cried out, 'Save me! save me!' That he rushed upon the wretches, two of whom fought him, sword in hand, whilst a third held the woman, and tried to stop her mouth; that he wounded one in the arm; and that the ruffians, hearing people pass at the end of the street, and fearing they might come to his assistance, fled; that he then went up to the lady, who told him that they were not robbers, but villains, one of whom was desperately in love with her; and that the lady knew not how to express her gratitude; that she had begged him not to follow her, after he had conducted her to a *fiacre*; that she would not tell him her name; but that she insisted on his accepting a little ring, as a token of remembrance; and that she promised to see him again, and to tell him her whole history, if he gave her his address: that he complied with this request of the

11—2

lady, whom he represented as a charming person, and who, in the overflowing of her gratitude, embraced him several times. This is all very fine, so far," said Madame d'Amblimont, "but hear the rest. The Marquis de —— exhibited himself everywhere the next day, with a black ribbon bound round his arm, near the wrist, in which part he said he had received a wound. He related his story to everybody, and everybody commented upon it after his own fashion. He went to dine with the Dauphin, who spoke to him of his bravery, and of his fair unknown, and told him that he had already complimented the Duke de C—— on the affair. I forgot to tell you," continued Madame d'Amblimont, "that, on the very night of the adventure, he called on Madame d'Estillac, an old gambler, whose house is open till four in the morning; that everybody there was surprised at the disordered state in which he appeared: that his bag-wig had fallen off, one skirt of his coat was cut, and his right hand bleeding. That they instantly bound it up, and gave him some Rota wine. Four days ago, the Duke de C—— supped with the King, and sat near M. de St. Florentin. He talked to him of his relation's adventure, and asked him if he had made any inquiries concerning the lady. M. de St. Florentin coldly answered, 'No:' and M. de C—— remarked, on asking him some further questions, that he kept his eyes fixed on his plate, looking embarrassed, and answered in monosyllables. He asked him the reason of this, upon which M. de Florentin told him that it was extremely distressing to him to see him under such a mistake. 'How can you know that, supposing it to be the fact,' said M. de ——.

' Nothing is more easy to prove,' replied M. de St. Florentin. ' You may imagine that, as soon as I was informed of the Marquis de ——'s adventure, I set on foot inquiries, the result of which was, that, on the night when this affair was said to have taken place, a party of the watch was set in ambuscade in this very street, for the purpose of catching a thief who was coming out of a gaming house ; that this party was there four hours, and heard not the slightest noise.' M. de C—— was greatly incensed at this recital, which M. de St. Florentin ought, indeed, to have communicated to the King. He has ordered, or will order, his relation to retire to his province.

" After this, you will judge, my dear, whether you were very likely to be graciously received when you went open-mouthed with your compliment to the Marchioness. This adventure," continued she, " reminded the King of one which occurred about fifteen years ago. The Count d'E——, who was what is called *enfant d'honneur* to the Dauphin, and about fourteen years of age, came into the Dauphin's apartments, one evening, with his bag-wig snatched off, and his ruffles torn, and said, that, having walked rather late near the piece of water *des Suisses*, he had been attacked by two robbers ; that he had refused to give them any-thing, drawn his sword, and put himself in an attitude of defence : that one of the robbers was armed with a sword, the other with a large stick, from which he had received several blows, but that he had wounded one in the arm, and that, hearing a noise at that moment, they had fled. But, unluckily for the little Count, it was known that people were on the spot at the precise time he mentioned, and had heard nothing. The Count was pardoned, on account of his youth. The Dauphin made him confess the truth, and it was looked upon as a childish freak, to set people talking about him."

The King disliked the King of Prussia, because he knew that the latter was in the habit of jesting upon his mistress, and the kind of life he led. It was Frederick's fault, as I have heard it said, that the King was not his most steadfast ally and friend, as much as sovereigns can be towards each other; but the jestings of Frederick had stung him, and made him conclude the treaty of Versailles. One day, he entered Madame's apartment with a paper in his hand, and said, "The King of Prussia is certainly a great man; he loves men of talent, and, like Louis XIV., he wishes to make Europe ring with his favours towards foreign *savans.* There is a letter from him, addressed to my Lord Mareschal,[1] ordering him to acquaint a *superieur* man of my kingdom (d'Alembert) that he has granted him a pension:" and, looking at the letter, he read the following words: "You must

1 George Keith, better known under the name of Milord Marshal, was the eldest son of William Keith, Earl Marshal of Scotland. He was an avowed partisan of the Stuarts, and did not lay down the arms he had taken up in their cause until it became utterly desperate, and drew upon its defenders useless dangers. When they were driven from their country, he renounced it, and took up his residence successively in France, Prussia, Spain, and Italy. The delicious country and climate of Valencia he preferred above any other.

Milord Marshal died in the month of May, 1778. It was he who said to Madame Geoffrin, speaking of his brother, who was field-marshal in the Prussian service, and died on the field of honour, "My brother leaves me the most glorious inheritance" (he had just laid the whole of Bohemia under contribution); "his property does not amount to seventy ducats." An eulogium on Milord Marshal, by d'Alembert, is extant. It is the most cruelly mangled of all his works, by Linguet — (*Vid. Annales Politiques,* 1778).

know that there is in Paris a man of the greatest merit, whose fortune is not proportionate to his talents and character. I may serve as eyes to the blind goddess, and repair in some measure the injustice, and I beg you to offer on that account. I flatter myself that he will accept this pension because of the pleasure I shall feel in obliging a man who joins beauty of character to the most sublime intellectual talents." The King here stopped, on seeing MM. de Ayen and de Gontaut enter, and then recommenced reading the letter to them, and added, " It was given me by the Minister for Foreign Affairs, to whom it was confided by Milord Mareschal, for the purpose of obtaining my permission for this *sublime genius* to accept the favour. But," said the King. "what do you think is the amount ? " Some said six, eight, ten thousand livres. " You have not guessed,"

said the King, "It is twelve hundred livres."—
"For sublime talents," said the Duke d'Ayen,
"it is not much. But the philosophers will make
Europe resound with this letter, and the King
of Prussia will have the pleasure of making a
great noise at little expense."

The Chevalier de Courten,[1] who had been in
Prussia, came in, and, hearing this story told,
said, " I have seen what is much better than
that : passing through a village in Prussia, I got
out at the post-house, while I was waiting for
horses ; and the Postmaster, who was a captain
in the Prussian service, showed me several letters
in Frederick's handwriting, addressed to his uncle,
who was a man of rank, promising him to provide
for his nephews ; the provision he made for this,

1 The Chevalier de Courten was a Swiss, and a man
of talent.

the eldest of these nephews, who was dreadfully
wounded, was the postmastership which he then
held." M. de Marigny related this story at
Quesnay's, and added, that the man of genius
above-mentioned was d'Alembert, and that the
King had permitted him to accept the pension.
He added, that his sister had suggested to the
King that he had better give d'Alembert a pension of twice the value, and forbid him to take
the King of Prussia's. This advice he would not
take, because he looked upon d'Alembert as an
infidel. M. de Marigny took a copy of the letter,
which he lent me.

A certain nobleman, at one time, affected to
cast tender glances on Madame Adelaïde. She
was wholly unconscious of it ; but, as there are
Arguses at Court, the King was, of course, told
of it. and, indeed, he thought he had perceived

it himself. I know that he came into Madame de Pompadour's room one day, in a great passion, and said, " Would you believe that there is a man in my Court insolent enough to dare to raise his eyes to one of my daughters ? " Madame had never seen him so exasperated, and this illustrious nobleman was advised to feign a necessity for visiting his estates. He remained there two months. Madame told me, long after, that she thought that there were no tortures to which the King would not have condemned any man who had seduced one of his daughters. Madame Adelaide, at the time in question, was a charming person, and united infinite grace, and much talent, to a most agreeable face.

A courier brought Madame de Pompadour a letter, on reading which she burst into tears. It contained the intelligence of the battle of Rosbach, which M. de Soubise sent her, with all the details. I heard her say to the Marshal de Belle-Isle, wiping her eyes, " M. de Soubise is inconsolable ; he does not try to excuse his conduct, he sees nothing but the disastrous fortune which pursues him."—" M. de Soubise must, however, have many things to urge in his own behalf," said M. de Belle-Isle, " and so I told the King." —" It is very noble in you, Marshal, not to suffer an unfortunate man to be overwhelmed ; the public are furious against him, and what has he done to deserve it?"—" There is not a more honourable nor a kinder man in the world. I only fulfil my duty in doing justice to the truth, and to a man for whom I have the most profound esteem. The King will explain to you, Madame, how that M. de Soubise was forced to give battle by the Prince of Saxe-Hildbourgshausen,[1] whose troops fled first,

---

1 Field-marshal of the Imperial army, November, 1757.

and carried along the French troops." Madame would have embraced the old Marshal if she had dared, she was so delighted with him.

M. de Soubise, having gained a battle,[1] was made Marshal of France: Madame was enchanted with her friend's success. But, either it was unimportant, or the public were offended at his promotion; nobody talked of it but Madame's friends. This unpopularity was concealed from her, and she said to Colin, her steward, at her toilet, "Are you not delighted at the victory M. de Soubise has gained? What does the public say of it? He has taken his revenge well." Colin was embarrassed, and knew not what to answer. As she pressed him further, he replied that he had been ill, and had seen nobody for a week.

M. de Marigny came to see me one day,

---

1 That of Lutzelberg, in October, 1758.

very much out of humour. I asked him the cause. "I have," said he, "just been intreating my sister not to make M. le Normand-de-Mezi Minister of the Marine. I told her that she was heaping coals of fire upon her own head. A favourite ought not to multiply the points of attack upon herself." The Doctor entered. "You," said the Doctor, "are worth your weight in gold, for the good sense and capacity you have shewn in your office, and for your moderation, but you will never be appreciated as you deserve; your advice is excellent; there will never be a ship taken but Madame will be held responsible for it to the public, and you are very wise not to think of being in the ministry yourself."

One day, when I was at Paris, I went to dine with the Doctor, who happened to be there at the same time; there were, contrary to his usual custom, a good many people, and, among others, a handsome young Master of the Requests, who took a title from some place, the name of which I have forgotten, but who was a son of M. Turgot, the *prévôt des marchands*. They talked a great deal about administration, which was not very amusing to me; they then fell upon the subject of the love Frenchmen bear to their kings. M. Turgot here joined in the conversation, and said, "This is not a blind attachment: it is a deeply rooted sentiment, arising from an indistinct recollection of great benefits. The French nation—I may go farther—Europe, and all mankind, owe to a King of France," (I have forgotten his name[1]) "whatever liberty they enjoy. He established *communes*, and conferred on an immense number of men a civil existence. I am

1 Philip the Long.

aware that it may be said, with justice, that
he served his own interests by granting these
franchises; that the cities paid him taxes, and
that his design was to use them as instruments
of weakening the power of the great nobles : but
what does that prove, but that this measure was
at once useful, politic, and humane ? " From
kings in general the conversation turned upon
Louis XV., and M. Turgot remarked that his
reign would be always celebrated for the advancement of the sciences, the progress of knowledge,
and of philosophy.   He added that Louis XV.
was deficient in the quality which Louis XIV.
possessed to excess; that is to say, in a good
opinion of himself; that he was well-informed ;
that nobody was more perfectly master of the
topography of France; that his opinion in the
council was always the most judicious; and that

it was much to be lamented that he had not
more confidence in himself, or that he did not
rely upon some minister who enjoyed the confidence of the nation.   Everybody agreed with
him.   I begged M. Quesnay to write down what
young Turgot had said, and showed it to Madame.
She praised this Master of the Requests greatly,
and spoke of him to the King.   "It is a good
breed," said he.

One day, I went out to walk, and saw,
on my return, a great many people going and
coming, and speaking to each other privately: it
was evident that something extraordinary had
happened.   I asked a person of my acquaintance
what was the matter.   "Alas!" said he, with
tears in his eyes, "some assassins, who had
formed the project of murdering the King, have
inflicted several wounds on a garde-du-corps, who

overheard them in a dark corridor: he is carried to the hospital: and as he has described the colour of these men's coats, the Police are in quest of them in all directions, and some people, dressed in clothes of that colour, are already arrested." I saw Madame with M. de Gontaut, and I hastened home. She found her door besieged by a multitude of people, and was alarmed: when she got in, she found the Count de Noailles. "What is all this, Count?" said she. He said he was come expressly to speak to her, and they retired to her closet together. The conference was not long. I had remained in the drawing-room, with Madame's equerry, the Chevalier de Sosent, Gourbillon, her valet-de-chambre, and some strangers. A great many details were related: but, the wounds being little more than scratches, and the garde-du-corps having let fall some contradictions, it was thought that he was an impostor, who had invented all this story to bring himself into favour. Before the night was over, this was proved to be the fact, and, I believe, from his own confession. The King came, that evening, to see Madame de Pompadour; he spoke of this occurrence with great *sang froid,* and said, " The gentleman who wanted to kill me was a wicked madman ; this is a low scoundrel."

When he spoke of Damiens, which was only while his trial lasted, he never called him anything but *that gentleman.*

I have heard it said that he proposed having him shut up in a dungeon for life ; but that the horrible nature of the crime made the judges insist upon his suffering all the tortures inflicted upon like occasions. Great numbers, many of them women, had the barbarous curiosity to witness the execution ; amongst others, Madame de P——, a very beautiful woman, and the wife of a farmer-general. She hired two places at a window for twelve louis, and played a game of cards in the room whilst waiting for the execution to begin. On this being told to the King, he covered his eyes with his hands, and exclaimed, " *Fi, la Vilaine!* " I have been told that she, and others, thought to pay their court in this way, and signalise their attachment to the King's person.

Two things were related to me by M. Duclos at the time of the attempt on the King's life.

The first, relative to the Count de Sponheim, who was Duke de Deux-Ponts, and next in succession to the Palatinate and Electorate of Bavaria. He was thought to be a great friend

to the King, and had made several long sojourns
in France. He came frequently to see Madame.
M. Duclos told us that the Duke de Deux-Ponts,
having learned, at Deux-Ponts, the attempt on
the King's life, immediately set out in a carriage
for Versailles : " But remark," said he, " the
spirit of *courtisancrie* of a prince, who may be
Elector of Bavaria and the Palatinate to-morrow.
This was not enough. When he arrived within
ten leagues of Paris, he put on an enormous
pair of jack-boots, mounted a post-horse, and
arrived in the court of the palace cracking his
whip. If this had been real impatience, and not
charlatanism, he would have taken horse twenty
leagues from Paris."—" I don't agree with you,"
said a gentleman whom I did not know : " impatience sometimes seizes one towards the end
of an undertaking, and one employs the readiest

means then in one's power. Besides, the Duke de Deux-Ponts might wish, by showing himself thus on horseback, to serve the King, to whom he is attached, by proving to Frenchmen how greatly he is beloved and honoured in other countries." Duclos resumed; "Well," said he, "do you know the story of M. de C——? The first day the King saw company, after the attempt of Damiens, M. de C—— pushed so vigorously through the crowd that he was one of the first to come into the King's presence; but he had on so shabby a black coat that it caught the King's attention, who burst out laughing, and said, 'Look at C——, he has had the skirt of his coat torn off.' M. de C—— looked as if he was only then first conscious of his loss, and said, 'Sire, there is such a multitude hurrying to see your Majesty, that I was obliged to fight my way through them, and, in the effort, my coat has been torn.' — 'Fortunately it was not worth much,' said the Marquis de Souvré, 'and you could not have chosen a worse one to sacrifice on the occasion.'

Madame de Pompadour had been very judiciously advised to get her husband, M. le Normand, sent to Constantinople, as ambassador. This would have a little diminished the scandal caused by seeing Madame de Pompadour, with the title of Marchioness, at Court, and her husband Farmer-General at Paris. But he was so attached to a Paris life, and to his opera habits, that he could not be prevailed upon to go. Madame employed a certain M. d'Arboulin, with whom she had been acquainted before she was at Court, to negotiate this affair. He applied to a Mademoiselle Rem,[1] who had been an opera-dancer, and who was M. le Normand's mistress. She made him very fine promises; but she was like him, and preferred a Paris life. She would do nothing in it.

At the time that plays were acted in the little apartments, I obtained a lieutenancy for one of my relations, by a singular means, which proves the value the greatest people set upon the slightest access to the Court. Madame did not like to ask anything of M. d'Argenson, and, being pressed by my family, who could not imagine that, situated as I was, it could be difficult for me to obtain a command for a good soldier, I determined to

[1] M. le Normand married this Mademoiselle *Rem*, according to the following epigram, which was much in vogue:

Pour réparer *miseriam*
Que Pompadour fit à la France,
Le Normand, plein de conscience,
Vient d'épouser *rempublicam*.

go and ask the Count d'Argenson. I made my
request, and presented my memorial. He received
me coldly, and gave me vague answers. I went
out, and the Marquis de V——, who was in
his closet, followed me. "You wish to obtain
a command," said he; "there is one vacant,
which is promised me for one of my protégés;
but if you will do me a favour in return, or
obtain one for me, I will give it to you. I
want to be a *police officer*, and you have it in your
power to get me a place." I told him I did
not understand the purport of his jest. " I will
tell you," said he: "*Tartuffe* is going to be acted
in the cabinets, and there is the part of a police
officer, which only consists of a few lines. Prevail upon Madame de Pompadour to assign me
that part, and the command is yours." I
promised nothing, but I related the history to

Madame, who said she would arrange it for me.
The thing was done, and I obtained the command, and the Marquis de V—— thanked Madame
as if she had made him a Duke.

The King was often annoyed by the Parliaments, and said a very remarkable thing concerning them, which M. de Gontaut repeated to
Doctor Quesnay in my presence. " Yesterday,"
said he, "the King walked up and down the
room with an anxious air. Madame de Pompadour asked him if he was uneasy about his health,
as he had been, for some time, rather unwell.
" No," replied he; " but I am greatly annoyed
by all these remonstrances."—" What can come
of them," said she, " that need seriously disquiet
Your Majesty? Are you not master of the Parliaments, as well as of all the rest of the
kingdom?"—" That is true," said the King;

" but, if it had not been for these counsellors and presidents, I should never have been stabbed by *that gentleman* " (he always called Damiens so). " Ah ! Sire," cried Madame de Pompadour. " Read the trial," said he : " It was the language of those gentlemen he names which turned his head." — " But," said Madame, " I have often thought, that if the Archbishop[1] could be sent to Rome——— " " Find anybody who will accomplish that business, and I will give him whatever he pleases." Quesnay said the King was right in all he had uttered. The Archbishop was exiled shortly after, and the King was seriously afflicted at being driven to take such a step. " What a pity," he often said, " that so excellent a man should be so obstinate."—"And so shallow," said somebody, one day. " Hold your

---

1 M. de Beaumont.

tongue," replied the King, somewhat sternly. The
Archbishop was very charitable, and liberal to
excess, but he often granted pensions without
discernment.[1] He granted one of an hundred
louis to a pretty woman, who was very poor,
and who assumed an illustrious name, to which

[1] The following is a specimen of the advantages taken
of his natural kindness. Madame la Caille, who acted the
Duennas at the Opéra Comique, was recommended to him
as the mother of a family, who deserved his protection.
The worthy prelate asked what he could do for her.
"Monseigneur," said the actress, "two words from your
hand to the Duke de Richelieu would induce him to grant
me a *demi-part*." M. de Beaumont, who was very little
acquainted with the language of the theatre, thought that
a *demi-part* meant a more liberal portion of the Marshal's
alms, and the note was written in the most pressing
manner. The Marshal answered, "that he thanked the
Archbishop for the interest he took in the Théatre Italien,
and in Madame la Caille, who was a very useful person
at that theatre; that, nevertheless, she had a bad voice;
but that the recommendation of the Archbishop was to be
preferred to the greatest talents, and that the *demi-part* was
granted."

she had no right. The fear lest she should be plunged into vice led him to bestow such excessive bounty upon her; and the woman was an admirable dissembler. She went to the Archbishop's, covered with a great hood, and, when she left him, she amused herself with a variety of lovers.

Great people have the bad habit of talking very indiscreetly before their servants. M. de Gontaut once said these words, covertly, as he thought, to the Duke de ——, " That measures had been taken which would, probably, have the effect of determining the Archbishop to go to Rome, with a Cardinal's hat; and that, if he desired it, he was to have a coadjutor."

A very plausible pretext had been found for making this proposition, and for rendering it flattering to the Archbishop, and agreeable to his

sentiments.   The affair had been very adroitly
begun, and success appeared certain.   The King
had the air, towards the Archbishop, of entire
unconsciousness of what was going on.   The
negotiator acted as if he were only following the
suggestions of his own mind, for the general good.
He was a friend of the Archbishop, and was very
sure of a liberal reward.   A valet of the Duke
de Gontaut, a very handsome young fellow, had
perfectly caught the sense of what was spoken in
a mysterious manner.   He was one of the lovers
of the lady of the hundred louis a year, and had
heard her talk of the Archbishop, whose relation
she pretended to be.   He thought he should
secure her good graces by informing her that
great efforts were being made to induce her patron
to reside at Rome, with a view to get him away
from Paris.   The lady instantly told the Arch-

bishop, as she was afraid of losing her pension if he went. The information squared so well with the negotiation then on foot, that the Archbishop had no doubt of its truth. He cooled, by degrees, in his conversations with the negotiator, whom he regarded as a traitor, and ended by breaking with him. These details were not known till long afterwards. The lover of the lady having been sent to the Bicêtre, some letters were found among his papers, which gave a scent of the affair, and he was made to confess the rest.

In order not to compromise the Duke de Gontaut, the King was told that the valet had come to a knowledge of the business from a letter which he had found in his master's clothes. The King took his revenge by humiliating the Archbishop, which he was enabled to do by means of the information he had obtained concerning the conduct of the lady, his protégée. She was found guilty of swindling, in concert with her beloved valet; but, before her punishment was inflicted, the Lieutenant of Police was ordered to lay before Monseigneur a full account of the conduct of his relation and pensioner. The Archbishop had nothing to object to in the proofs which were submitted to him; he said, with perfect calmness, that she was not his relation; and, raising his hands to heaven, "She is an unhappy wretch," said he, "who has robbed me of the money which was destined for the poor. But God knows that, in giving her so large a pension, I did not act lightly. I had, at that time, before my eyes the example of a young woman who once asked me to grant her seventy pounds a year, promising me that she would always live very virtuously, as she had hitherto done. I refused her, and she said, on leaving me, ' I must turn to the left. Monseigneur, since the way on the right is closed against me.' The unhappy creature has kept her word but too well. She found means of establishing a pharo-table at her house, which is tolerated; and she joins, to the most profligate conduct in her own person, the infamous trade of a corrupter of youth; her house is the abode of every vice. Think, Sir, after that, whether it was not an act of prudence, on my part, to grant the woman in question a pension, suitable to the rank in which I thought her born, to prevent her abusing the gifts of youth, beauty, and talents, which she possessed, to her own perdition, and the destruction of others." The Lieutenant of Police told the King that he was touched with the candour and the noble simplicity of the prelate. " I never doubted his virtues," replied the King, " but I wish he would be quiet." This same Archbishop gave a pension of fifty pounds a year to the greatest scoundrel in Paris. He is a poet,[1] who writes abominable verses: this pension is granted on condition that his poems are never printed. I learned this fact from M. de Marigny, to whom he recited some of his horrible verses one evening, when he supped with him, in company with some people of quality. He chinked the money in his

---

[1] Robbé de Beauveset, celebrated, or, at least, known, for his impious and licentious verses. His filthy life corresponded with his cynical writings. He reformed, in some degree, towards the middle of his life, in consequence of the persuasions of the Count d'Autré, who was, at that time, very pious, but ceased to be so after he had converted Robbé. " I shall work out my salvation as I serve in the militia," said he, " by substitute."

Robbé died at St. Germaine, in 1794; his verses are to be found in several collections, but have never been published together.

pocket : "This is my good Archbishop's," said he, laughing; "I keep my word with him : my poem will not be printed during my life, but I read it. What would the good prelate say if he knew that I shared my last quarter's allowance with a charming little opera-dancer ? 'It is the Arch- bishop, then, who keeps me,' said he to me ; 'Oh la! how droll that is!'" The King heard this, and was much scandalised at it. "How difficult it is to do good!" said he.

The King came into Madame de Pompadour's room, one day, as she was finishing dressing. "I have just had a strange adventure," said he : "would you believe, that, in going out of my wardroom into my bedroom, I met a gentleman face to face?"—"My God! Sire," cried Madame, terrified. "It was nothing," replied he : "but I confess I was greatly surprised : the man appeared speechless with consternation. ' What do you do here ? ' said I, civilly. He threw himself on his knees, saying, ' Pardon me, Sire; and, above all, have me searched.' He instantly emptied his pockets himself; he pulled off his coat in the greatest agitation and terror: at last, he told me, that he was cook to ——, and a friend of Beccari, whom he came to visit; that he had mistaken the staircase, and, finding all the doors open, he had wandered into the room in which I found him, and which he would have instantly left : I rang; Guimard came, and was astonished enough at finding me tête-à-tête with a man in his shirt. He begged Guimard to go with him into another room, and to search his whole person. After this, the poor devil returned, and put on his coat. Guimard said to me, ' He is certainly an honest man, and tells the truth;

this may, besides, be easily ascertained.' Another of the servants of the palace came in, and happened to know him. ' I will answer for this good man,' said he, ' who, moreover, makes the best *bœuf à l'écarlate* in the world.' As I saw the man was so agitated that he could not stand steady, I took fifty louis out of my bureau, and said, ' Here, Sir, are fifty louis, to quiet your alarms.' He went out, after throwing himself at my feet." Madame exclaimed on the impropriety of having the King's bedroom thus accessible to everybody. He talked with great calmness of this strange apparition, but it was evident that he controlled himself, and that he had, in fact, been much frightened, as, indeed, he had reason to be. Madame highly approved of the gift : and she was the more right in applauding it, as it was by no means in the King's usual manner.

M. de Marigny said, when I told him of this adventure, that he would have wagered a thousand louis against the King's making a present of fifty, if anybody but I had told him of the circumstance. "It is a singular fact," continued he, "that all of the race of Valois have been liberal to excess; this is not precisely the case with the Bourbons, who are rather reproached with avarice. Henry IV. was said to be avaricious. He gave to his mistresses, because he could refuse them nothing; but he played with the eagerness of a man whose whole fortune depends on the game. Louis XIV. gave through ostentation. It is most astonishing," added he, "to reflect on what might have happened. The King might actually have been assassinated in his chamber, without anybody knowing anything of the matter and without a possibility of discovering the murderer." For more than a fortnight Madame could not get over this incident.

About that time she had a quarrel with her brother, and both were in the right. Proposals were made to him to marry the daughter of one of the greatest noblemen of the Court, and the King consented to create him a duke, and even to make the title hereditary. Madame was right in wishing to aggrandise her brother, but he declared that he valued his liberty above all things, and that he would not sacrifice it except for a person he really loved. He was a true Epicurean philosopher, and a man of great capacity, according to the report of those who knew him well, and judged him impartially. It was entirely at his option to have had the reversion of M. de St. Florentin's place, and the place of Minister of Marine, when M. de Machault retired: he said to

his sister, at the time, " I spare you many vexations, by depriving you of a slight satisfaction.
The people would be unjust to me, however well
I might fulfil the duties of my office.   As to M.
de St. Florentin's place, he may live five-and-
twenty years, so that I should not be the better
for it.   Kings' mistresses are hated enough on
their own account ; they need not also draw upon
themselves the hatred which is directed against
ministers."   M. Quesnay repeated this conversation to me.

The King had another mistress, who gave
Madame de Pompadour some uneasiness.   She
was a woman of quality, and the wife of one of
the most assiduous courtiers.

A man in immediate attendance on the King's
person, and who had the care of his clothes,
came to me one day, and told me that, as he was

very much attached to Madame, because she was
good and useful to the King, he wished to inform
me, that a letter having fallen out of the pocket
of a coat which His Majesty had taken off, he
had had the curiosity to read it, and found it to
be from the Countess de ——, who had already
yielded to the King's desires.   In this letter, she
required the King to give her fifty thousand
crowns in money, a regiment for one of her relations, and a bishopric for another, and to dismiss
Madame in the space of fifteen days, &c.   I
acquainted Madame with what this man told me,
and she acted with singular greatness of mind.
She said to me, " I ought to inform the King of
this breach of trust of his servant, who may, by
the same means, come to the knowledge of, and
make a bad use of, important secrets ; but I feel
a repugnance to ruin the man : however, I cannot

permit him to remain near the King's person, and here is what I shall do—Tell him that there is a place of ten thousand francs a-year vacant in one of the provinces; let him solicit the Minister of Finance for it, and it shall be granted to him; but, if he should ever disclose through what interest he has obtained it, the King shall be made acquainted with his conduct. By this means, I think I shall have done all that my attachment and duty prescribe. I rid the King of a faithless domestic, without ruining the individual." I did as Madame ordered me: her delicacy and address inspired me with admiration. She was not alarmed on account of the lady, seeing what her pretensions were. "She drives too quick," remarked Madame, "and will certainly be overturned on the road." The lady died.

"See what the Court is; all is corruption

there, from the highest to the lowest," said I to Madame, one day, when she was speaking to me of some facts that had come to my knowledge. " I could tell you many others," replied Madame: " but the little chamber, where you often remain, must furnish you with a sufficient number." This was a little nook, from whence I could hear a great part of what passed in Madame's apartment. The Lieutenant of Police sometimes came secretly to this apartment, and waited there. Three or four persons, of high consideration, also found their way in, in a mysterious manner, and several devotees, who were, in their hearts, enemies of Madame de Pompadour. But these men had not petty objects in view: one required the government of a province; another, a seat in the council; a third, a Captaincy of the Guards: and this man would have obtained it if the Maréchale de

Mirepoix had not requested it for her brother, the
Prince of Beauvau.   The Chevalier du Muy was
not among these apostates; not even the promise
of being High Constable would have tempted him
to make up to Madame, still less to betray his
master, the Dauphin.   This prince was, to the last
degree, weary of the station he held.   Sometimes,
when teased to death by ambitious people, who
pretended to be Catos, or wonderfully devout, he
took part against a minister against whom he was
prepossessed :   then relapsed into his accustomed
state of inactivity and ennui.   .

The King used to say, " My son is lazy ; his
temper is Polonese—hasty and changeable ; he
has no tastes ; he cares nothing for hunting, for
women, or for good living ; perhaps he imagines
that if he were in my place he would be happy ;
at first, he would make great changes, create

everything anew, as it were. In a short time he would be as tired of the rank of King as he now is of his own : he is only fit to live *en philosophe,* with clever people about him." The King added, " He loves what is right : he is truly virtuous, and does not want understanding."

M. de St. Germain said, one day, to the King, " To think well of mankind, one must be neither a Confessor, nor a Minister, nor a Lieutenant of Police."—" Nor a King," said His Majesty. "Ah ! Sire," replied he, " you remember the fog we had a few days ago, when we could not see four steps before us. Kings are commonly surrounded by still thicker fogs, collected around them by men of intriguing character, and faithless ministers :— all, of every class, unite in endeavouring to make things appear to Kings in any light but the true one." I heard this from the mouth of the famous

Count de St. Germain, as I was attending upon Madame, who was ill in bed. The King was there ; and the Count, who was a welcome visitor, had been admitted. There were also present, M. de Gontaut, Madame de Brancas, and the Abbé de Bernis. I remember, that the very same day, after the Count was gone out, the King talked in a style which gave Madame great pain. Speaking of the King of Prussia, he said, " That is a madman, who will risk all to gain all, and may, perhaps, win the game, though he has neither religion, morals, nor principles. He wants to make a noise in the world, and he will succeed. Julian, the Apostate, did the same."—" I never saw the King so animated before," observed Madame, when he was gone out ; " and really the comparison with Julian, the Apostate, is not amiss, considering the irreligion of the King of Prussia.

If he gets out of his perplexities, surrounded as he is by his enemies, he will be one of the greatest men in history."

M. de Bernis remarked, " Madame is correct in her judgment, for she has no reason to pronounce his praises ; nor have I, though I agree with what she says." Madame de Pompadour never enjoyed so much influence as at the time when M. de Choiseul became one of the ministry. From the time of the Abbé de Bernis she had afforded him her constant support, and he had been employed in foreign affairs, of which he was said to know but little. Madame made the Treaty of Vienna, though the first idea of it was certainly furnished her by the Abbé. I have been informed by several persons that the King often talked to Madame upon this subject ; for my own part, I never heard any conversation relative to

14

it, except the high praises bestowed by her on the Empress and the Prince de Kaunitz, whom she had known a good deal of. She said that he had a clear head, the head of a statesman. One day, when she was talking in this strain, someone tried to cast ridicule upon the Prince on account of the style in which he wore his hair, and the four valets de chambre, who made the hair-powder fly in all directions, while Kaunitz ran about that he might only catch the superfine part of it. "Aye," said Madame, "just as Alcibiades cut off his dog's tail in order to give the Athenians something to talk about, and to turn their attention from those things he wished to conceal."

Never was the public mind so inflamed against Madame de Pompadour as when news arrived of the battle of Rosbach. Every day she received anonymous letters, full of the grossest abuse; atrocious verses, threats of poison and assassination. She continued long a prey to the most acute sorrow, and could get no sleep but from opiates. All this discontent was excited by her protecting the Prince of Soubise; and the Lieutenant of Police had great difficulty in allaying the ferment of the people. The King affirmed that it was not his fault. M. du Verney[1] was the confidant of Madame in everything relating to war; a subject which he well understood, though not a military man by profession. The old Marshal de Noailles called him, in derision, the General of the flour, but Marshal Saxe, one day, told Madame that du Verney knew more of military matters than the old Marshal. Du Verney once paid a visit to Madame de Pompadour, and

[1] Brother of M. de Montmartel, and a man of great talent.

found her in company with the King, the Minister of War, and two Marshals; he submitted to them the plan of a campaign, which was generally applauded. It was through his influence that M. de Richelieu was appointed to the command of the army, instead of the Marshal d'Estrées. He came to Quesnay two days after, when I was with him. The Doctor began talking about the art of war, and I remember he said, " Military men make a great mystery of their art : but what is the reason that young Princes have always the most brilliant success ? Why, because they are active and daring. When Sovereigns command their troops in person what exploits they perform ! Clearly, because they are at liberty to run all risks." These observations made a lasting impression on my mind.

The first physician came, one day, to see Madame : he was talking of madmen and madness.

The King was present, and everything relating to disease of any kind interested him. The first physician said that he could distinguish the symptoms of approaching madness six months beforehand. "Are there any persons about the Court likely to become mad?" said the King. "I know one who will be imbecile in less than three months," replied he. The King pressed him to tell the name. He excused himself for some time. At last he said, "It is M. de Séchelles, the Controller-General."—"You have a spite against him," said Madame, "because he would not grant you what you asked."—"That is true," said he, "but though that might possibly incline me to tell a disagreeable truth, it would not make me invent one. He is losing his intellects from debility. He affects gallantry at his age, and I perceive the connection in his ideas is becoming feeble and irregular." The King laughed ; but three months afterwards he came to Madame, saying, " Séchelles gives evident proofs of dotage in the Council. We must appoint a successor to him." Madame de Pompadour told me of this on the way to Choisy. Some time afterwards, the first physician came to see Madame, and spoke to her in private. " You are attached to M. Berryer, Madame," said he, " and I am sorry to have to warn you that he will be attacked by madness, or by catalepsy, before long. I saw him this morning at chapel, sitting on one of those very low little chairs, which are only meant to kneel upon. His knees touched his chin. I went to his house after mass : his eyes were wild, and when his secretary spoke to him, he said, ' *Hold your tongue, pen. A pen's business is to write, and not to speak.*' " Madame, who liked the Keeper of the Seals, was very much concerned, and begged the first physician not to mention what he had perceived. Four days after this, M. Berryer was seized with catalepsy, after having talked incoherently. This is a disease which I did not know even by name, and got it written down for me. The patient remains in precisely the same position in which the fit seizes him : one leg or arm elevated, the eyes wide open, or just as it may happen. This latter affair was known to all the Court at the death of the Keeper of the Seals.

When the Marshal de Belle-Isle's son was killed in battle, Madame persuaded the King to pay his father a visit. He was rather reluctant, and Madame said to him, with an air half angry, half playful :

———— " Barbare ! dont l'orgueil
Croit le sang d'un sujet trop payé d'un coup d'œil."

The King laughed, and said, " Whose fine verses are those ? "—" Voltaire's," said Madame ———. " As barbarous as I am, I gave him the place of gentleman in ordinary, and a pension," said the King.

The King went in state to call on the Marshal, followed by all the Court ; and it certainly appeared that this solemn visit consoled the Marshal for the loss of his son, the sole heir[1] to his name.

When the Marshal died, he was carried to his house on a common hand-barrow, covered with a shabby cloth. I met the body. The bearers were laughing and singing. I thought it was some servant, and asked who it was. How great was my surprise at learning that these were the

1 The Marshal bequeathed a part of his fortune to the King.

remains of a man abounding in honours and in riches. Such is the Court ; the dead are always in fault, and cannot be put out of sight too soon.

The King said, " M. Fouquet is dead, I hear." " He was no longer Fouquet," replied the Duke d'Ayen ; " Your Majesty had permitted him to change that name, under which, however, he acquired all his reputation." The King shrugged his shoulders. His Majesty had, in fact, granted him letters patent, permitting him not to sign Fouquet during his ministry. I heard this on the occasion in question. M. de Choiseul had the war department at his death. He was every day more and more in favour. Madame treated him with greater distinction than any previous minister, and his manners towards her were the most agreeable it is possible to conceive, at once respectful and gallant. He never passed a day

without seeing her. M. de Marigny could not
endure M. de Choiseul, but he never spoke of
him, except to his intimate friends. Calling, one
day, at Quesnay's, I found him there. They were
talking of M. de Choiseul. " He is a mere *petit
maître*," said the Doctor, " and, if he were handsomer, just fit to be one of Henry the Third's
favourites." The Marquis de Mirabeau and M.
de la Rivière came in. "This kingdom," said
Mirabeau, "is in a deplorable state. There is
neither national energy, nor the only substitute
for it—money." " It can only be regenerated,"
said la Rivière, "by a conquest, like that of
China, or by some great internal convulsion; but
woe to those who live to see that! The French
people do not do things by halves." These words
made me tremble, and I hastened out of the
room. M. de Marigny did the same, though

without appearing at all affected by what had been said.—" You heard de la Rivière," said he, —" but don't be alarmed, the conversations that pass at the Doctor's are never repeated; these are honourable men, though rather chimerical. They know not where to stop. I think, however, they are in the right way; only, unfortunately, they go too far." I wrote this down immediately.

The Count de St. Germain came to see Madame de Pompadour, who was ill, and lay on the sofa. He shewed her a little box, containing topazes, rubies, and emeralds. He appeared to have enough to furnish a treasury. Madame sent for me to see all these beautiful things. I looked at them with an air of the utmost astonishment, but I made signs to Madame that I thought them all false. The Count felt for something in a pocket-book, about twice as large as a spectacle-case, and, at length, drew out two or three little paper packets, which he unfolded, and exhibited a superb ruby. He threw on the table, with a contemptuous air, a little cross of green and white stones. I looked at it and said, "That is not to be despised." I put it on, and admired it greatly. The Count begged me to accept it, I refused—he urged me to take it. Madame then refused it for me. At length, he pressed it upon me so warmly that Madame, seeing that it could not be worth above forty pounds, made me a sign to accept it. I took the cross, much pleased at the Count's politeness; and, some days after, Madame presented him with an enamelled box, upon which was the portrait of some Grecian sage, (whose name I don't recollect), to whom she compared him. I shewed the cross to a jeweller, who valued it at sixty-five pounds. The Count offered to bring Madame some enamel portraits, by Petitot, to look at, and she told him to bring them after dinner, while the King was hunting. He shewed his portraits, after which Madame said to him, " I have heard a great deal of a charming story you told two days ago, at supper, at M. le Premier's, of an occurrence you witnessed fifty or sixty years ago." He smiled and said, " It is rather long." " So much the better," said she, with an air of delight. Madame de Gontaut and the ladies came in, and the door was shut ; Madame made a sign to me to sit down behind the screen. The Count made many apologies for the ennui which his story would, perhaps, occasion. He said, " Sometimes, one can tell a story pretty well ; at other times it is quite a different thing."

" At the beginning of this century, the
Marquis de St. Gilles was Ambassador from
Spain to the Hague. In his youth he had been
particularly intimate with the Count de Moncade,
a grandee of Spain, and one of the richest nobles
of that country. Some months after the Marquis's
arrival at the Hague, he received a letter from
the Count, entreating him, in the name of their
former friendship, to render him the greatest
possible service. ' You know,' said he, ' my dear
Marquis, the mortification I felt that the name
of Moncade was likely to expire with me. At
length, it pleased heaven to hear my prayers,
and to grant me a son: he gave early promise
of dispositions worthy of his birth, but he, some
time since, formed an unfortunate and disgraceful
attachment to the most celebrated actress of the
company of Toledo. I shut my eyes to this

imprudence on the part of a young man whose conduct had, till then, caused me unmingled satisfaction. But, having learnt that he was so blinded by passion as to intend to marry this girl, and that he had even bound himself by a written promise to that effect, I solicited the King to have her placed in confinement. My son, having got information of the steps I had taken, defeated my intentions by escaping with the object of his passion. For more than six months I have vainly endeavoured to discover where he has concealed himself, but I have now some reason to think he is at the Hague.' The Count earnestly conjured the Marquis to make the most rigid search, in order to discover his son's retreat, and to endeavour to prevail upon him to return to his home. 'It is an act of justice,' continued he, 'to provide for the girl, if she consents to give up the written promise of marriage which she has received, and I leave it to your discretion to do what is right for her, as well as to determine the sum necessary to bring my son to Madrid in a manner suitable to his condition. I know not,' concluded he, 'whether you are a father; if you are, you will be able to sympathise in my anxieties.' The Count subjoined to his letter an exact description of his son. and the young woman by whom he was accompanied. On the receipt of this letter, the Marquis lost not a moment in sending to all the inns in Amsterdam, Rotterdam, and the Hague, but in vain—he could find no trace of them. He began to despair of success, when the idea struck him that a young French page of his, remarkable for his quickness and intelligence, might be employed with advantage. He promised to reward

him handsomely if he succeeded in finding the
young woman, who was the cause of so much
anxiety, and gave him the description of her
person. The page visited all the public places
for many days, without success; at length, one
evening, at the play, he saw a young man and
woman, in a box, who attracted his attention.
When he saw that they perceived he was looking
at them, and withdrew to the back of the box to
avoid his observation, he felt confident that they
were the objects of his search. He did not take
his eyes from the box, and watched every move-
ment in it. The instant the performance ended,
he was in the passage leading from the boxes to
the door, and he remarked that the young man,
who, doubtless, observed the dress he wore, tried
to conceal himself, as he passed him, by putting
his handkerchief before his face. He followed

him, at a distance, to the inn called the *Vicomte de Turenne*, which he saw him and the woman enter; and, being now certain of success, he ran to inform the Ambassador. The Marquis de St. Gilles immediately repaired to the inn, wrapped in a cloak, and followed by his page and two servants. He desired the landlord to show him to the room of a young man and woman, who had lodged for some time in his house. The landlord, for some time, refused to do so, unless the Marquis would give their name. The page told him to take notice that he was speaking to the Spanish Ambassador, who had strong reasons for wishing to see the persons in question. The innkeeper said, they wished not to be known, and that they had absolutely forbidden him to admit anybody into their apartment who did not ask for them by name; but that, since the

Ambassador desired it, he would show him their room. He then conducted them up to a dirty, miserable garret. He knocked at the door, and waited for some time; he then knocked again pretty loudly, upon which the door was half-opened. At the sight of the Ambassador and his suite, the person who opened it immediately closed it again, exclaiming that they had made a mistake. The Ambassador pushed hard against him, forced his way in, made a sign to his people to wait outside, and remained in the room. He saw before him a very handsome young man, whose appearance perfectly corresponded with the description, and a young woman, of great beauty, and remarkably fine person, whose countenance, form, colour of the hair, &c., were also precisely those described by the Count de Moncade. The young man spoke first. He complained of the violence used in breaking into the apartment of a stranger, living in a free country, and under the protection of its laws. The Ambassador stepped forward to embrace him, and said, ' It is useless to feign, my dear Count ; I know you, and I do not come here to give pain to you or to this lady, whose appearance interests me extremely.' The young man replied, that he was totally mistaken ; that he was not a Count, but the son of a merchant of Cadiz ; that the lady was his wife ; and, that they were travelling for pleasure. The Ambassador, casting his eyes round the miserably-furnished room, which contained but one bed, and some packages of the shabbiest kind, lying in disorder about the room, ' Is this, my dear child (allow me to address you by a title which is warranted by my tender regard for your father), is this a fit residence for the son

of the Count de Moncade ? ' The young man still
protested against the use of any such language,
as addressed to him. At length, overcome by
the entreaties of the Ambassador, he confessed,
weeping, that he was the son of the Count de
Moncade, but declared, that nothing should induce
him to return to his father, if he must abandon
a woman he adored. The young woman burst
into tears, and threw herself at the feet of the
Ambassador, telling him, that she would not be
the cause of the ruin of the young Count ; and
that generosity, or rather, love, would enable her
to disregard her own happiness, and, for his sake,
to separate herself from him. The Ambassador
admired her noble disinterestedness. The young
man, on the contrary, received her declaration
with the most desperate grief. He reproached
his mistress, and declared, that he would never

abandon so estimable a creature, nor suffer the sublime generosity of her heart to be turned against herself. The Ambassador told him, that the Count de Moncade was far from wishing to render her miserable, and that he was commissioned to provide her with a sum sufficient to enable her to return into Spain, or to live where she liked. Her noble sentiments, and genuine tenderness, he said, inspired him with the greatest interest for her, and would induce him to go to the utmost limits of his powers, in the sum he was to give her ; that he, therefore, promised her ten thousand florins, that is to say, about twelve hundred pounds, which would be given her the moment she surrendered the promise of marriage she had received, and the Count de Moncade took up his abode in the Ambassador's house, and promised to return to Spain. The young woman seemed perfectly indifferent to the sum proposed, and wholly absorbed in her lover, and in the grief of leaving him. She seemed insensible to everything but the cruel sacrifice which her reason, and her love itself, demanded. At length, drawing from a little portfolio the promise of marriage, signed by the Count, 'I know his heart too well,' said she, 'to need it.' Then she kissed it again and again, with a sort of transport, and delivered it to the Ambassador, who stood by, astonished at the grandeur of soul he witnessed. He promised her, that he would never cease to take the liveliest interest in her fate, and assured the Count of his father's forgiveness. 'He will receive with open arms,' said he, 'the prodigal son, returning to the bosom of his distressed family; the heart of a father is an exhaustless mine of tenderness. How great will be the felicity of my friend on the receipt of these tidings, after his long anxiety and affliction; how happy do I esteem myself, at being the instrument of that felicity.' Such was, in part, the language of the Ambassador, which appeared to produce a strong impression on the young man. But, fearing lest, during the night, love should regain all his power, and should triumph over the generous resolution of the lady, the Marquis pressed the young Count to accompany him to his hotel. The tears, the cries of anguish, which marked this cruel separation, cannot be described; they deeply touched the heart of the Ambassador, who promised to watch over the young lady. The Count's little baggage was not difficult to remove, and, that very evening, he was installed in the finest apartment of the Ambassador's house. The Marquis was overjoyed at having restored to the

illustrious house of Moncade the heir of its greatness, and of its magnificent domains. On the
following morning, as soon as the young Count
was up, he found tailors, dealers in cloth, lace,
stuffs, &c., out of which he had only to choose.
Two valets de chambre, and three laquais, chosen
by the Ambassador for their intelligence and good
conduct, were in waiting in his ante-chamber, and
presented themselves, to receive his orders. The
Ambassador shewed the young Count the letter
he had just written to his father, in which he con-
gratulated him on possessing a son whose noble
sentiments and striking qualities were worthy of his
illustrious blood, and announced his speedy return.
The young lady was not forgotten ; he confessed,
that to her generosity he was partly indebted for
the submission of her lover, and expressed his
conviction that the Count would not disapprove

the gift he had made her, of ten thousand florins.
That sum was remitted, on the same day, to this
noble and interesting girl, who left the Hague
without delay. The preparations for the Count's
journey were made; a splendid wardrobe, and an
excellent carriage were embarked at Rotterdam,
in a ship bound for France, on board which a
passage was secured for the Count, who was to
proceed from that country to Spain. A considerable sum of money, and letters of credit on
Paris, were given him at his departure; and the
parting between the Ambassador and the young
Count was most touching. The Marquis de
St. Gilles awaited with impatience the Count's
answer, and enjoyed his friend's delight by
anticipation. At the expiration of four months,
he received this long expected letter. It would
be utterly impossible to describe his surprise on

reading the following words, 'Heaven, my dear Marquis, never granted me the happiness of becoming a father, and, in the midst of abundant wealth and honours, the grief of having no heirs, and seeing an illustrious race end in my person, has shed the greatest bitterness over my whole existence. I see, with extreme regret, that you have been imposed upon by a young adventurer, who has taken advantage of the knowledge he had, by some means, obtained, of our old friendship. But your Excellency must not be the sufferer. The Count de Moncade is, most assuredly, the person whom you wished to serve; he is bound to repay what your generous friendship hastened to advance, in order to procure him a happiness which he would have felt most deeply. I hope, therefore, Marquis, that your Excellency will have no hesitation in accepting the remittance contained in this letter, of three thousand louis of France, of the disbursal of which you sent me an account.'"

The manner in which the Count de St. Germain spoke, in the characters of the young adventurer, his mistress, and the Ambassador, made his audience weep and laugh by turns. The story is true in every particular, and the adventurer surpasses Gusman d'Alfarache in address, according to the report of some persons present. Madame de Pompadour thought of having a play written, founded on this story; and the Count sent it to her in writing, from which I transcribed it.

M. Duclos came to the Doctor's, and harangued with his usual warmth. I heard him saying to two or three persons, "People are unjust to great men, Ministers and Princes; nothing, for

instance, is more common than to undervalue
their intellect. I astonished one of these little
gentlemen of the corps of the *infallibles*, by telling
him that I could prove that there had been
more men of ability in the house of Bourbon,
for the last hundred years, than in any other
family."—"You prove that?" said somebody,
sneeringly. "Yes," said Duclos; "and I will
tell you how. The great Condé, you will allow,
was no fool; and the Duchess de Longueville
is cited as one of the wittiest women that ever
lived. The Regent was a man who had few
equals, in every kind of talent and acquirement.
The Prince de Conti, who was elected King of
Poland, was celebrated for his intelligence, and,
in poetry, was the successful rival of La Fare
and St. Aulaire. The Duke of Burgundy was
learned and enlightened. His Duchess, the

daughter of Louis XIV., was remarkably clever, and wrote epigrams and couplets. The Duke du Maine is generally spoken of only for his weakness, but nobody had a more agreeable wit. His wife was mad, but she had an extensive acquaintance with letters, good taste in poetry, and a brilliant and inexhaustible imagination. Here are instances enough, I think," said he; "and, as I am no flatterer, and hate to appear one, I will not speak of the living." His hearers were astonished at this enumeration, and all of them agreed in the truth of what he had said. He added, " Don't we daily hear of *silly d'Argen-son,*[1] because he has a good-natured air, and a

---

[1] René Louis d'Argenson, who was Minister for Foreign Affairs. He was the author of *Considérations sur le Gouvernement*, and of several other works, from which succeeding political writers have drawn, and still draw ideas, which they give to the world as new. This man, remarkable not only for profound and original thinking,

bourgeois tone? and yet, I believe, there have not been many ministers comparable to him in knowledge and in enlightened views." I took a pen, which lay on the Doctor's table, and begged M. Duclos to repeat to me all the names he had mentioned, and the eulogium he had bestowed on each. "If," said he, "you show that to the Marchioness, tell her how the conversation arose, and that I did not say it in order that it might come to her ears, and eventually, perhaps, to those of another person. I am an historiographer, and I will render justice,

but for clear and forcible expression, was, nevertheless, *d'Argenson la bête.* It is said, however, that he affected the simplicity, and, even silliness of manner, which procured him that appellation. If, as we hope, the unedited memoirs left by René d'Argenson will be given to the world, they will be found fully to justify the opinion of Duclos, with regard to this Minister, and the inappropriateness of his nickname.

but I shall, also, often inflict it."—"I will answer
for that," said the Doctor, "and our master
will be represented as he really is. Louis XIV.
liked verses, and patronised poets; that was very
well, perhaps, in his time, because one must
begin with something; but this age will be
very superior to the last. It must be acknowledged that Louis XV., in sending astronomers
to Mexico and Peru, to measure the earth, has a
higher claim to our respect than if he directed
an opera. He has thrown down the barriers
which opposed the progress of philosophy, in
spite of the clamour of the devotees: the Ency-
clopædia will do honour to his reign." Duclos,
during this speech, shook his head. I went away,
and tried to write down all I had heard, while it
was fresh. I had the part which related to the
Princes of the Bourbon race copied by a valet,

who wrote a beautiful hand, and I gave it to Madame de Pompadour. But she said to me, "What! is Duclos an acquaintance of yours? Do you want to play the bel esprit, my dear good woman? That will not sit well upon you." The truth is, that nothing can be further from my inclination. I told her, that I met him accidentally at the Doctor's, where he generally spent an hour when he came to Versailles. "The King knows him to be a worthy man," said she.

Madame de Pompadour was ill, and the King came to see her several times a day. I generally left the room when he entered, but, having stayed a few minutes, on one occasion, to give her a glass of chicory water, I heard the King mention Madame d'Egmont. Madame raised her eyes to heaven, and said, "That name always recalls to me a most melancholy and barbarous affair: but

16

it was not my fault." These words dwelt in my mind, and, particularly, the tone in which they were uttered. As I stayed with Madame till three o'clock in the morning, reading to her a part of the time, it was easy for me to try to satisfy my curiosity. I seized a moment, when the reading was interrupted, to say, " You looked dreadfully shocked, Madame, when the King pronounced the name of d'Egmont." At these words, she again raised her eyes, and said, " You would feel as I do, if you knew the affair."—" It must, then, be deeply affecting, for I do not think that it personally concerns you, Madame."—" No," said she, " it does not; as, however, I am not the only person acquainted with this history, and as I know you to be discreet, I will tell it you. The last Count d'Egmont married a reputed daughter of the Duke de Villars; but the Duchess had never lived with her husband, and the Countess d'Egmont is, in fact, a daughter of the Chevalier d'Orleans.[1] At the death of her husband, young, beautiful, agreeable, and heiress to an immense fortune, she attracted the suit and homage of all the most distinguished men at Court. Her mother's director, one day, came into her room, and requested a private interview : he then revealed to her that she was the offspring of an adulterous intercourse, for which her mother had been doing penance for five-and-twenty years. ' She could not,' said he, ' oppose your former marriage, although it caused her extreme distress. Heaven did not grant you children : but, if you marry again, you run the risk, Madame, of transmitting to another family the immense wealth, which does not, in fact, belong to you, and which is the price of crime.'

[1] Legitimate son of the Regent, Grand Prior of France.

" The Countess d'Egmont heard this recital with horror. At the same instant, her mother entered, and, on her knees, besought her daughter to avert her eternal damnation. Madame d'Egmont tried to calm her own and her mother's mind. 'What can I do?' said she, to her. 'Consecrate yourself wholly to God,' replied the director, 'and thus expiate your mother's crime.' The Countess, in her terror, promised whatever they asked, and proposed to enter the Carmelites. I was informed of it, and spoke to the King about the barbarous tyranny the Duchess de Villars and the director were about to exercise over this unhappy young woman : but we knew not how to prevent it. The King, with the utmost kindness, prevailed on the Queen to offer her the situation of Lady of the Palace, and desired the Duchess's friends to persuade her to endeavour to deter her daughter from becoming a Carmelite. It was all in vain; the wretched victim was sacrificed."

Madame took it into her head to consult a fortune-teller, called Madame Bontemps, who had told M. de Bernis' fortune, as I have already related, and had surprised him by her predictions. M. de Choiseul, to whom she mentioned the matter, said that the woman had also foretold fine things that were to happen to him. "I know it," said she, "and, in return, you promised her a carriage, but the poor woman goes on foot still." Madame told me this, and asked me how she could disguise herself, so as to see the woman without being known. I dared not propose any scheme then, for fear it should not succeed; but, two days after, I talked to her surgeon about the art, which some beggars practise, of counterfeiting sores, and altering their features. He said that was easy enough. I let the thing drop, and, after an interval of some minutes, I said, " If one could change one's features, one might have great diversion at the opera, or at balls. What alterations would it be necessary to make in me, now, to render it impossible to recognise me?" "In the first place," said he, "you must alter the colour of your hair, then you must have a false nose, and put a spot on some part of your face, or a wart, or a few hairs." I laughed, and said, "Help me to contrive this for the next ball; I have not been to one for twenty years: but I am dying to puzzle somebody, and to tell him things which no one but I can tell him. I shall come home, and go to bed, in a quarter of an hour."—" I must take the measure of your nose," said he; "or do you take it with wax, and I will have a nose made: you can get a flaxen or brown wig." I repeated to Madame what the surgeon had told me : she was delighted at it. I took the measure of her nose, and of my own, and carried them to the surgeon, who, in two days, gave me the two noses, and a wart, which Madame stuck under her left eye, and some paint for the eyebrows. The noses were most delicately made, of a bladder, I think, and these, with the other disguises, rendered it impossible to recognise the face, and yet did not produce any shocking appearance. All this being accomplished, nothing remained but to give notice to the fortune-teller; we waited for a little excursion to Paris, which Madame was to take, to look at her house. I then got a person, with whom I had no connection, to speak to a waiting-woman of the Duchess of Rufféc, to obtain an interview with the woman. She made some difficulty, on account of the police ; but we promised secrecy, and appointed the place of meeting. Nothing could be more contrary to Madame de Pompadour's character, which was one of extreme timidity, than to engage in such an adventure. But her curiosity was raised to the highest pitch, and, moreover, everything was so well arranged that there was not the slightest risk. Madame had let M. de Gontaut, and her valet de chambre, into the secret. The latter had hired two rooms for his niece, who was then ill, at Versailles, near Madame's hotel. We went out in the evening, followed by the valet de chambre, who was a safe man, and by the Duke, all on foot. We had not, at farthest, above two hundred steps to go. We were shown into two small rooms, in which were fires. The two men remained in one, and we in the other. Madame had thrown herself on a sofa. She had on a night-cap, which concealed half her face, in an unstudied manner. I was near the fire, leaning on a table, on which were two candles. There were lying on the chairs, near us, some clothes, of small value. The fortune-teller rang — a little servant girl let her in, and then went to wait in the room where the gentlemen were. Coffee-cups, and a coffee-pot, were set; and I had taken care to place, upon a little buffet, some cakes, and a bottle of Malaga wine, having heard that Madame Bontemps assisted her inspiration with that liquor. Her face, indeed, sufficiently proclaimed it. "Is that lady ill?" said she, seeing Madame de Pompadour stretched languidly on the sofa. I told her that she would soon be better, but that she had kept her room for a week. She heated the coffee, and prepared

the two cups, which she carefully wiped, observ-
ing that nothing impure must enter into this
operation. I affected to be very anxious for a
glass of wine, in order to give our oracle a pretext for assuaging her thirst, which she did, without much entreaty. When she had drunk two or
three small glasses (for I had taken care not to
have large ones), she poured the coffee into one
of the two large cups. "This is yours," said
she; "and this is your friend's; let them stand
a little." She then observed our hands and our
faces; after which she drew a looking-glass from
her pocket, into which she told us to look, while
she looked at the reflections of our faces. She
next took a glass of wine, and immediately threw
herself into a fit of enthusiasm, while she in-
spected my cup, and considered all the lines
formed by the dregs of the coffee she had poured

out. She began by saying. *"That is well— prosperity—but there is a black mark—distresses. A man becomes a comforter. Here, in this corner, are friends, who support you. Ah! who is he that persecutes them? But justice triumphs — after rain, sunshine—a long journey successful. There, do you see these little bags? That is money which has been paid—to you, of course, I mean. That is well. Do you see that arm?"—"Yes:"* "*That is an arm supporting something: a woman veiled: I see her; it is you. All this is clear to me. I hear, as it were, a voice speaking to me. You are no longer attacked. I see it, because the clouds in that direction are passed off* (pointing to a clearer spot). *But, stay—I see small lines which branch out from the main spot. These are sons, daughters, nephews — that is pretty well.*" She appeared overpowered with the effort she was making. At length, she added, *"That is *all.   You have had good luck first—misfortune after-ward.   You have had a friend, who has exerted him-self with success to extricate you from it.   You have had law-suits—at length fortune has been reconciled to you, and will change no more."*   She drank another glass of wine.   " Your health, Madame," said she to the Marchioness, and went through the same ceremonies with the cup.   At length, she broke out, *" Neither fair nor foul.   I see there, in the distance, a serene sky ; and then all these things that appear to ascend—all these things are applauses.   Here is a grave man, who stretches out his arms.   Do you see ? — look attentively."* — *" That is true,"* said Madame de Pompadour, with surprise (there was, indeed, some appearance of the kind).   *" He points to something square—that is an open coffer.   Fine weather.—But, look ! there are clouds of azure and gold, which surround you.   Do you see that ship on the high sea ? How favourable the wind is ! You are on board; you land in a beautiful country, of which you become the Queen. Ah! what do I see ? Look there — look at that hideous, crooked, lame man, who is pursuing you—but he is going on a fool's errand. I see a very great man, who supports you in his arms. Here, look! he is a kind of giant. There is a great deal of gold and silver—a few clouds here and there. But you have nothing to fear. The vessel will be sometimes tossed about, but it will not be lost.—Dixi."* Madame said, " When shall I die, and of what disease ? " — " I never speak of that," said she : " *see here, rather— but fate will not permit it.—I will shew you how fate confounds everything,"* — shewing her several confused lumps of the coffee-dregs. " Well, never mind as to the time, then, only tell me the kind of death." The fortune-teller looked in the cup,

and said, " *You will have time to prepare yourself.*"
I gave her only two louis, to avoid doing anything
remarkable.   She left us, after begging us to keep
her secret, and we rejoined the Duke de Gontaut,
to whom we related everything that had passed.
He laughed heartily, and said, " Her coffee-dregs
are like the clouds—you may see what you please
in them."

There was one thing in my horoscope which
struck me, that was the comforter ; because one
of my uncles had taken great care of me, and had
rendered me the most essential services.   It is
also true that I afterwards had an important law-
suit ; and, lastly, there was the money which had
come into my hands through Madame de Pompadour's patronage and bounty.   As for Madame,
her husband was represented accurately enough
by the man with the coffer : then the country of

which she became Queen seemed to relate to her
present situation at Court ; but the most remarkable thing was the crooked and lame man, in
whom Madame thought she recognised the Duke
de V----, who was very much deformed. Madame
was delighted with her adventure and with her
horoscope, which she thought corresponded very
remarkably with the truth. Two days after, she
sent for M. de St. Florentin, and begged him not
to molest the fortune-teller. He laughed, and
replied that he knew why she interceded for this
woman. Madame asked him why he laughed.
He related every circumstance of her expedition
with astonishing exactness[1]; but he knew nothing
of what had been said, or, at least, so he pretended. He promised Madame that, provided

---

1 M. de St. Florentin was Minister for Paris, to whom
the Lieutenant of Police was accountable.

Bontemps did nothing which called for notice, she should not be obstructed in the exercise of her profession, especially if she followed it in secret. " I know her," added he, "and I, like other people, have had the curiosity to consult her. She is the wife of a soldier in the guards. She is a clever woman in her way, but she drinks. Four or five years ago, she got such hold on the mind of Madame de Ruffée, that she made her believe she could procure her an elixir of beauty, which would restore her to what she was at twenty-five. The Duchess pays high for the drugs of which this elixir is compounded; and sometimes they are bad: sometimes, the sun, to which they were exposed, was not powerful enough; sometimes, the influence of a certain constellation was wanting. Sometimes, she has the courage to assure the Duchess that she really is grown handsomer, and actually succeeds in making her believe it." But the history of this woman's daughter is still more curious. She was exquisitely beautiful, and the Duchess brought her up in her own house. Bontemps predicted to the girl, in the Duchess's presence, that she would marry a man of two thousand a-year. This was not very likely to happen to the daughter of a soldier in the guards. It did happen, nevertheless. The little Bontemps married the President Beaudouin, who was mad. But, the tragical part of the story is, that her mother had also foretold that she would die in child-birth of her first child, and that she did actually die in child-birth, at the age of eighteen, doubtless under a strong impression of her mother's prophecy, to which the improbable event of her marriage had given such extraordinary weight.

17

Madame told the King of the adventure her
curiosity had led her into, at which he laughed,
and said he wished the police had arrested
her. He added a very sensible remark. " In
order to judge," said he, " of the truth or falsehood of such predictions, one ought to collect
fifty of them. It would be found that they are
almost always made up of the same phrases,
which are sometimes inapplicable, and sometimes
hit the mark. But the first are rarely mentioned, while the others are always insisted on."

I have heard, and, indeed, it is certainly true,
that M. de Bridge lived on terms of intimacy with
Madame, when she was Madame d'Etioles. He
used to ride on horseback with her, and, as he
is so handsome a man that he has retained the
name of *the handsome man*, it was natural enough
that he should be thought the lover of a very

handsome woman. I have heard something more
than this. I was told that the King said to
M. de Bridge, "Confess, now, that you were her
lover. She has acknowledged it to me, and I exact
from you this proof of sincerity." M. de Bridge
replied, that Madame de Pompadour was at liberty
to say what she pleased for her own amusement,
or for any other reason; but that he, for his part,
could not assert a falsehood; that he had been
her friend; that she was a charming companion,
and had great talents; that he delighted in her
society; but that his intercourse with her had
never gone beyond the bounds of friendship. He
added, that her husband was present in all their
parties, that he watched her with a jealous eye,
and that he would not have suffered him to be
so much with her if he had conceived the least
suspicion of the kind. The King persisted, and

17—2

told him he was wrong to endeavour to conceal a fact which was unquestionable.   It was rumoured, also, that the Abbé de Bernis had been a favoured lover of hers.   The said Abbé was rather a cox-comb; he had a handsome face, and wrote poetry. Madame de Pompadour was the theme of his gallant verses.   He sometimes received the com-pliments of his friends upon his success with a smile which left some room for conjecture, although he denied the thing in words.   It was, for some time, reported at Court that she was in love with the Prince de Beauvau: he is a man distinguished for his gallantries, his air of rank and fashion, and his high play; he is brother to the little Maréchale: for all these reasons, Madame is very civil to him, but there is nothing marked in her behaviour.   She knows, besides, that he is in love with a very agreeable woman.

Now that I am on the subject of lovers, I cannot avoid speaking of M. de Choiseul. Madame likes him better than any of those I have just mentioned, but he is not her lover. A lady, whom I know perfectly well, but whom I do not choose to denounce to Madame, invented a story about them, which was utterly false. She said, as I have good reason to believe, that one day, hearing the King coming, I ran to Madame's closet door; that I coughed in a particular manner; and, that the King having, happily, stopped a moment to talk to some ladies, there was time to adjust matters, so that Madame came out of the closet with me and M. de Choiseul, as if we had been all three sitting together. It is very true that I went in to carry something to Madame, without knowing that the King was come, and that she came out of the closet with M. de Choiseul, who had a paper in his hand, and that I followed her a few minutes after. The King asked M. de Choiseul what that paper was which he had in his hand; he replied that it contained the remonstrance from the Parliament.

Three or four ladies witnessed what I now relate, and as, with the exception of one, they were all excellent women, and greatly attached to Madame, my suspicions could fall on none but the one in question, whom I will not name, because her brother has always treated me with great kindness. Madame de Pompadour had a lively imagination and great sensibility, but nothing could exceed the coldness of her temperament. It would, besides, have been extremely difficult for her, surrounded as she was, to keep up an intercourse of that kind with any man. It is true that this difficulty would have been diminished

in the case of an all-powerful minister, who had
constant pretexts for seeing her in private. But
there was a much more decisive fact—M. de
Choiseul had a charming mistress—the Princess
de R——, and Madame knew it, and often spoke
of her. He had, besides, some remains of liking
for the Princess de Kinski, who followed him from
Vienna. It is true that he soon after discovered
how ridiculous she was. All these circumstances
combined were, surely, sufficient to deter Madame
from engaging in a love affair with the Duke;
but his talents and agreeable qualities captivated
her. He was not handsome, but he had manners
peculiar to himself, an agreeable vivacity, a delightful gaiety; this was the general opinion of his
character. He was much attached to Madame,
and though this might, at first, be inspired by a
consciousness of the importance of her friendship

to his interest, yet, after he had acquired sufficient
political strength to stand alone, he was not the
less devoted to her, nor less assiduous in his
attentions. He knew her friendship for me, and
he one day said to me, with great feeling, " I am
afraid, my dear Madame du Hausset, that she
will sink into a state of complete dejection, and
die of melancholy—Try to divert her." What a
fate for the favourite of the greatest monarch in
existence ! thought I.

One day, Madame de Pompadour had retired
to her closet with M. Berryer. Madame d'Amblimont stayed with Madame de Gontaut, who called
me to talk about my son. A moment after, M. de
Gontaut came in and said, " d'Amblimont, who
shall have the Swiss guards ? "—" Stop a moment,"
said she ; " let me call my council——, M. de
Choiseul."—" That is not so very bad a thought,"

said M. de Gontaut, "but I assure you, you are the first person who has suggested it." He immediately left us, and Madame d'Amblimont said, " I'll lay a wager he is going to communicate my idea to M. de Choiseul." He returned very shortly, and, M. Berryer having left the room, he said to Madame de Pompadour, "A singular thought has entered d'Amblimont's head."—"What absurdity now?" said Madame.—"Not so great an absurdity neither," said he. "She says the Swiss guards ought to be given to M. de Choiseul, and, really, if the King has not positively promised M. de Soubise, I don't see what he can do better."—"The King has promised nothing," said Madame, "and the hopes I gave him were of the vaguest kind. I only told him it was possible. But though I have a great regard for M. de Soubise, I do not think his merits comparable to those of M. de Choiseul." When the King came in, Madame, doubtless, told him of this suggestion. A quarter of an hour afterwards, I went into the room to speak to her, and I heard the King say, " You will see that, because the Duke du Maine, and his children, had that place, he will think he ought to have it, on account of his rank as Prince (Soubise); but Marshal de Bassompierre was not a Prince; and, by the bye, the Duke de Choiseul is his grand-nephew; do you know that?"—" Your Majesty is better acquainted with the history of France than anybody," replied Madame. Two days after this, Madame de —— said to me, " I have two great delights: M. de Soubise will not have the Swiss guards, and Madame de Marsan will be ready to burst with rage at it; this is the first: and M. de Choiseul will have them; this is the greatest."

[1] There was an universal talk of a young lady with whom the King was as much in love as it was possible for him to be. Her name was Romans. She was said to be a charming girl. Madame de Pompadour knew of the King's visits, and her confidantes brought her most alarming reports of the affair. The Maréchale de Mirepoix, who had the best head in Madame's council, was the only one who encouraged her. "I do not tell you," said she, "that he loves you better than her; and if she could be transported hither by the stroke of a fairy's wand; if she could entertain him this evening at supper: if she were familiar with all his tastes, there would, perhaps, be sufficient reason for you to tremble for your power. But princes are, above all, pre-eminently the slaves of habit. The King's attachment to you

---

1 The whole of this passage is in a different hand-writing.

is like that he bears to your apartment, your furniture. You have formed yourself to his manners and habits; you know how to listen and reply to his stories; he is under no constraint with you; he has no fear of *boring* you. How do you think he could have resolution to uproot all this in a day, to form a new establishment, and to make a public exhibition of himself by so striking a change in his arrangements ?"—The young lady became pregnant; the reports current among the people, and even those at Court, alarmed Madame dreadfully. It was said that the King meant to legitimate the child, and to give the mother a title. "All that," said Madame de Mirepoix, "is in the style of Louis XIV.—such dignified proceedings are very unlike those of our master." Mademoiselle Romans lost all her influence over the King by her indiscreet boasting. She was even treated with harshness and violence, which were in no degree instigated by Madame. Her house was searched, and her papers seized; but the most important, those which substantiated the fact of the King's paternity, had been withdrawn. At length she gave birth to a son, who was christened under the name of Bourbon, son of Charles de Bourbon, Captain of Horse. The mother thought the eyes of all France were fixed upon her, and beheld in her son a future Duke du Maine. She suckled him herself, and she used to carry him in a sort of basket to the Bois de Boulogne. Both mother and child were covered with the finest laces. She sat down upon the grass in a solitary spot, which, however, was soon well known, and there gave suck to her royal babe. Madame had great curiosity to see her, and took me, one day, to the manufactory at

Sèvres, without telling me what she projected.
After she had bought some cups, she said, "I
want to go and walk in the Bois de Boulogne,"
and gave orders to the coachman to stop at a
certain spot where she wished to alight. She
had got the most accurate directions, and when
she drew near the young lady's haunt she gave
me her arm, drew her bonnet over her eyes, and
held her pocket handkerchief before the lower
part of her face. We walked, for some minutes,
in a path, from whence we could see the lady
suckling her child. Her jet black hair was turned
up, and confined by a diamond comb. She looked
earnestly at us. Madame bowed to her, and
whispered to me, pushing me by the elbow,
" Speak to her." I stepped forward, and exclaimed,
" What a lovely child ! " — " Yes, Madame," replied she, " I must confess that he is, though I

am his mother." Madame, who had hold of my arm, trembled, and I was not very firm. Mademoiselle Romans said to me, " Do you live in this neighbourhood ? "—" Yes, Madame," replied I, " I live at Auteuil with this lady, who is just now suffering from a most dreadful tooth-ache." — " I pity her sincerely, for I know that tormenting pain well." I looked all around, for fear anyone should come up who might recognise us. I took courage to ask her whether the child's father was a handsome man. " Very handsome, and, if I told you his name, you would agree with me."—" I have the honour of knowing him, then, Madame ?"— " Most probably you do." Madame, fearing, as I did, some rencontre, said a few words in a low tone, apologizing for having intruded upon her, and we took our leave. We looked behind us, repeatedly, to see if we were followed, and got into the carriage without being perceived. " It must be confessed that both mother and child are beautiful creatures," said Madame,—" not to mention the father; the infant has his eyes. If the King had come up while we were there, do you think he would have recognised us?"—" I don't doubt that he would, Madame, and then what an agitation I should have been in, and what a scene would it have been for the bystanders! and, above all, what a surprise to her!" In the evening, Madame made the King a present of the cups she had bought, but she did not mention her walk, for fear Mademoiselle Romans should tell him that two ladies, who knew him, had met her there such a day. Madame de Mirepoix said to Madame, " Be assured, the King cares very little about children; he has enough of them, and he will not be troubled with the mother or the son. See what sort of notice he takes of the Count de L——, who is strikingly like him. He never speaks of him, and I am convinced that he will never do anything for him. Again and again I tell you, we do not live under Louis XIV." Madame de Mirepoix had been Ambassadress to London, and had often heard the English make this remark.

Some alterations had been made in Madame de Pompadour's rooms, and I had no longer, as heretofore, the niche in which I had been permitted to sit, to hear Caffarelli, and, in later times, Mademoiselles Fel and Jeliotte. I, therefore, went more frequently to my lodgings in town, where I usually received my friends: more particularly when Madame visited her little hermitage, whither M. de Gontaut commonly accompanied her. Madame du Chiron, the wife of the

18

Head Clerk in the War-office, came to see me. "I feel," said she, "greatly embarrassed, in speaking to you about an affair, which will, perhaps, embarrass you also. This is the state of the case. A very poor woman, to whom I have sometimes given a little assistance, pretends to be a relation of the Marchioness de Pompadour. Here is her petition." I read it, and said that the woman had better write directly to Madame, and that I was sure, if what she asserted was true, her application would be successful. Madame du Chiron followed my advice. The woman wrote she was in the lowest depth of poverty, and I learnt that Madame sent her six pounds until she could gain more accurate information as to the truth of her story. Colin, who was commissioned to take the money, made inquiries of M. de Malvoisin, a relation of Madame, and a very respectable officer. The fact was found to be as she had stated it. Madame then sent her a hundred pounds, and promised her a pension of sixty pounds a year. All this was done with great expedition, and Madame had a visit of thanks from her poor relation, as soon as she had procured decent clothes to come in. That day the King happened to come in at an unusual hour, and saw this person going out. He asked who it was. " It is a very poor relation of mine," replied Madame. " She came, then, to beg for some assistance ?"—" No," said she.—" What did she come for then ?"—" To thank me for a little service I have rendered her," said she, blushing from the fear of seeming to boast of her liberality. "Well," said the King; " since she is your relation, allow me to have the pleasure of serving her too. I will give her fifty pounds a year out of my private purse, and, you know, she may send for the first year's allowance to-morrow." Madame burst into tears, and kissed the King's hand several times. She told me this three days afterwards, when I was nursing her in a slight attack of fever. I could not refrain from weeping myself at this instance of the King's kindness. The next day, I called on Madame du Chiron to tell her of the good fortune of her protegée ; I forgot to say that, after Madame had related the affair to me, I told her what part I had taken in it. She approved my conduct, and allowed me to inform my friend of the King's goodness. This action, which showed no less delicate politeness towards her than sensibility to the sufferings of the poor woman, made a deeper impression on Madame's heart than a pension of two thousand a year given to herself.

Madame had terrible palpitations of the heart.

Her heart actually seemed to leap. She consulted several physicians. I recollect that one of them made her walk up and down the room, lift a weight, and move quickly. On her expressing some surprise, he said, " I do this to ascertain whether the organ is diseased; in that case motion quickens the pulsation ; if that effect is not produced, the complaint proceeds from the nerves." I repeated this to my oracle, Quesnay. He knew very little of this physician, but he said his treatment was that of a clever man. His name was Rénard; he was scarcely known beyond the Marais. Madame often appeared suffocated, and sighed continually. One day, under pretence of presenting a petition to M. de Choiseul, as he was going out, I said, in a low voice, that I wished to see him a few minutes on an affair of importance to my mistress. He told me to come as soon as I pleased, and that I should be admitted. I told him that Madame was extremely depressed ; that she gave way to distressing thoughts, which she would not communicate ; that she, one day, said to me, " The fortune teller told me I *should have time to prepare myself* : I believe it, for I shall be worn to death by melancholy." M. de Choiseul appeared much affected ; he praised my zeal, and said that he had already perceived some indications of what I told him : that he would not mention my name, but would try to draw from her an explanation. I don't know what he said to her : but, from that time, she was much more calm. One day, but long afterwards, Madame said to M. de Gontaut, " I am generally thought to have great influence, but if it were not for M. de Choiseul, I should not be able to obtain a Cross of St. Louis."

The King and Madame de Pompadour had a very high opinion of Madame de Choiseul. Madame said, "She always says the right thing in the right place." Madame de Grammont was not so agreeable to them: and I think that this was to be attributed, in part, to the sound of her voice, and to her blunt manner of speaking: for she was said to be a woman of great sense, and devotedly attached to the King and Madame de Pompadour. Some people pretended that she tried to captivate the King, and to supplant Madame: nothing could be more false, or more ridiculously improbable. Madame saw a great deal of these two ladies, who were extremely attentive to her. She one day remarked to the Duke d'Ayen,[1] that M. de Choiseul was very fond of his sisters. "I know it, Madame," said he,

---

[1] Afterwards Marshal de Noailles.

"and many sisters are the better for that."—
"What do you mean?" said she.—"Why," said
he, "as the Duke de Choiseul loves his sister, it
is thought fashionable to do the same: and I know
silly girls, whose brothers formerly cared nothing
about them, who are now most tenderly beloved.
No sooner does their little finger ache, than their
brothers are running about to fetch physicians
from all corners of Paris. They flatter themselves that somebody will say, in M. de Choiseul's
drawing-room. "How passionately M. de ——
loves his sister: he would certainly die if he had
the misfortune to lose her." Madame related this
to her brother, in my presence, adding, that she
could not give it in the Duke's comic manner.
M. de Marigny said, "I have had the start of
them all, without making so much noise; and my
dear little sister knows that I loved her tenderly

before Madame de Grammont left her convent.
The Duke d'Ayen, however, is not very wrong;
he has made the most of it in his lively manner,
but it is partly true." — "I forgot," replied
Madame, "that the Duke said, 'I want extremely
to be in the fashion, but which sister shall I
take up? Madame de Caumont is a devil incar-
nate, Madame de Villars drinks, Madame d'Ar-
magnac is a bore, Madame de la Marck is half
mad.'"—"These are fine family portraits, Duke,"
said Madame. The Duke de Gontaut laughed,
during the whole of this conversation, im-
moderately. Madame repeated it, one day, when
she kept her bed. M. de G—— also began to
talk of his sister, Madame du Roure. I think, at
least, that is the name he mentioned. He was
very gay, and had the art of creating gaiety.
Somebody said, he is an excellent piece of furni-

ture for a favourite. He makes her laugh, and
asks for nothing either for himself or for others :
he cannot excite jealousy, and he meddles in
nothing. He was called the White Eunuch.
Madame's illness increased so rapidly that we
were alarmed about her : but bleeding in the foot
cured her as if by a miracle. The King watched
her with the greatest solicitude ; and I don't know
whether his attentions did not contribute as much
to the cure as the bleeding. M. de Choiseul remarked, some days after, that she appeared in
better spirits. I told him that I thought this
improvement might be attributed to the same
cause.

THE END

www.ingramcontent.com/pod-product-compliance
Lightning Source LLC
Chambersburg PA
CBHW020859020726
47497CB00005B/1478